West of Death

A CRAZY COZY MURDER MYSTERY

DR. CATHERINE GOTTFRED

B.T. GOTTFRED

Saturday Morning

COFFEE
WITH
DETECTIVE BLUE

6:09 AM

Chapter One

"Athena West?" A man in a gray suit asked as he stepped into the hotel's back office. I had been waiting here for two hours. My phone died fourteen minutes in. This was not going to go well.

"That's meeeeeeee." Extending vowels after one question. I'm doomed.

"I'm Detective Blue," he said as he sat in the chair across from me. A thin beige table between us. Our knees could almost touch. Even worse, I wanted them to.

"Are you sad, Detective Blue?" I asked, playing with the double meaning of his name to lighten the mood.

He insisted it stay heavy: "You work here at the resort?"

"Sorta." I should note I'm thirty-four years old and only talk like an air-headed teenager when I'm nervous. Or depressed. Or smitten. Or sugar deprived. At the moment, I might be all of the above.

"Either yes you work here or no you don't."

"Good point. Right. So... Elizabeth — "

"The victim?"

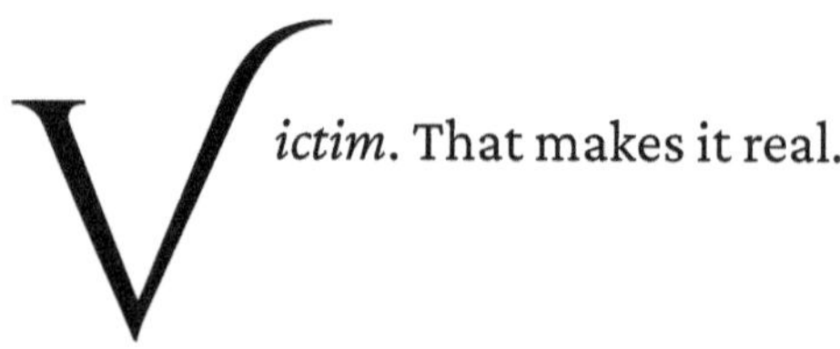

ictim. That makes it real.

"*M*s. West?"

"Yes, Elizabeth Diaz. Elizabeth is... was... the manager here at the resort. She's... was... my friend... sorta... We went to high school together and she asked me to come stay here a few days to observe."

"Observe what?" Detective Blue asked. He's got a mustache. I hate kissing men with mustaches. But he doesn't need to know that. Yet.

I should answer his question. But also *not* answer his question. 87% sure that Elizabeth was the only one who knew what she asked me to observe. And she was dead. "She never specified."

"Was she paying you to observe this never speci-fied thing?"

"She gave me a room and resort credit."

"So this was a favor?"

"I didn't think so. Do you think so? I mean, I just got fired *and* dumped so maybe, yeah, Elizabeth might have been doing me a favor by..."

"I was asking if you were doing a favor for Eliza-beth by coming here to — never mind. What job were you fired from?"

"Is that relevant?"

"Just answer the question, Ms. West."

"I'm a... was a kindergarten teacher."

"Why were you fired?"

"For reading a book."

"What book?"

"Jacob's New Dress." Off his confusion, I said, "It's about a boy who wears a dress to school."

"Why would a school fire you for that?"

"Detective, I appreciate your naiveté of the modern day fascist's objectives."

· · ·

Okay, maybe I could kiss him despite the mustache. Detective Blue had broad shoulders that could carry small boats and soft cheeks that could hold the hard corners of my weary head.

"Ms. West?"

"Huh?"

"Can you answer my question?"

"What question?"

"Ms. West, your inability to pay attention leads me to believe you're not taking the situation seriously."

"Sorry," I said and then realized I had kissed many men with mustaches and many black men but I had never kissed a black man with a mustache. So I'd probably say yes if he asked me out after he was done asking questions. Mostly because he's not a fascist but also because he's adorable when he gets frustrated with me. I've always thought I should marry someone who's adorable when they're frustrated with me. Because that probably meant he found me adorable when I was being frustrating. And I was frustrating a lot. Like *a lot.*

. . .

"MS. WEST!" The detective yelled. No one's adorable when they yell.

"Sorry. Maybe I'm nervous?"

"Did you know the victim's husband?"

"Travis?"

"Yes, Travis Diaz."

"Sorta." This sorta was *sorta* not true.

"Ms. West." He knew more than he was pretending not to know.

"Travis also went to high school with Elizabeth and me."

Detective Blue waited me out.

"Okay, Travis was *also* my high school boyfriend."

"And he cheated on you."

"Yeeeeah."

"Cheated on you *with* Elizabeth."

"Yeaaaaaaaaah."

"Mr. Diaz showed us some letters you sent to him and his wife in the years since the break up."

"Oh."

Detective Blue's eyes got very serious. A *little* adorable. But also a little scary. "Ms. West, I need you to stop obstructing my investigation."

"Am I a suspect? I am. Wow. Fascinating. I mean, not fascinating in a cool way. *So* not cool. It's just

I've never been a suspect in anything before. Do people usually ask for lawyers when they're suspects?"

"That's your constitutional right. Yes."

"Would *you* ask for a lawyer if you were me?"

Blue smiled this tiny, tiny smile as if I was being clever. Maybe I was. Sometimes I'm so clever I out-clever myself.

So I explained, "You, as an upstanding and studied officer of the law, would never need a lawyer. But I've only read books and seen movies about these sort of situations so maybe you could offer me some friendly advice."

Even as I reached behind me to scoop a yellow notepad off the filing cabinet and a light blue sharpie I had spotted on the floor, Detective Blue held silent. Probably smart. I'm an over-sharer.

For example, I couldn't stop myself from saying, "Probably easier for us to get to know each other without a lawyer, right? Right. So. First, I sent those letters to Elizabeth and Travis while I was in college and in a very dramatic phase of my life. Second, I believe, in these letters, I stated their trail of betrayal would be the death of both of them... not that I would be the one that would actually kill either of them. Three... wait, have you read *Confessions of a Teenage Broken Heart*?"

"The Netflix series?"

"It was a book first."

Detective Blue looked down at his notes. "Right. Right. Elizabeth and Travis wrote it together."

"No, *I* wrote it... and Travis sorta helped..."

"That's not what my notes say."

"Because they stole it from me."

"Ms. West, are you confessing you had more than one motive to kill Ms. Diaz?"

I wasn't very good at this. Jotted down my first notes on the yellow notepad. About Elizabeth. About Detective Blue's mustache. Then drew flowers with big petals. I like drawing flowers. Though I was about as good at drawing flowers as I was at feigning innocence.

"Ms. West, what are you writing down?"

"You can call me Athena."

W as I flirting with him? I was. I'm the type of person that believes you can meet your soul mate anytime, anywhere. Why eliminate the possibility of true love just because the circumstances were not ideal or the timing was bad?

"Ms. West."

(The timing of meeting Detective Blue definitely wasn't great... and the circumstances probably couldn't be worse.)

"Did you kill Elizabeth Diaz?"

"I mean... sorta?"

PART ONE

THE BIG DEATH AND THE FIVE SUSPECTS

Thursday Night

aka
35 HOURS and 44 MINUTES
BEFORE SAID
COFFEE
WITH
DETECTIVE BLUE

Chapter Two

My mother was in the middle of her speech of shame: "*By the time I was your age*, I had an eight year old girl, a ten year old boy, a four thousand square foot house, and had been promoted to manager at Marshall Fields even though..." Her usual pause.

I finished for her, "...you had only re-entered the work force eleven months before."

Mom stood back up from my eight *hundred* square foot apartment's only couch, stepped over my dramatically splayed body on the floor, and into the kitchen. "Athena, I don't tell you this so you can make fun of me."

"You say it to make me feel worse about my life than I already do."

"I *say it* to inspire you to make changes in your life."

"I got fired and dumped today, mother. I'm definitely making changes!" Laughed because I already tried crying.

"Do you have any tea?"

"Tea is gross."

"It's better for you than coffee. Especially the sugary lattes you call coffee but really are just dessert for breakfast."

"Mom, why are you here?"

"Because you called me up crying and I wanted to be here for you."

Nancy West was not a bad mother. She ended every conversation with an 'I love you' and a hug of genuine warmth. But the cost of those words and that embrace was high. If she had been born thirty years later or to progressive parents — or unloving conservative parents she was forced to rebel from — my mother would probably have been a Senator or a CEO of a Fortune Five Hundred company. Instead she dropped out of college to marry the handsome son of a rich man and be a mother and homemaker. If dad had never cheated on her, she probably wouldn't have worked a day in her life. But she retired last year as Macy's midwest regional manager with savings from shrewd investments that would be the envy of any hedge fund.

When my mother didn't say anything once inside my kitchen, I extracted myself from the floor. Boxes of cookies needed to be saved from a premature death. Mom was at the table, hiding her guilt with a book of sudoku opened in front of her. I knew better and fetched my double stuffed Oreos from the trash.

"You're never going to find a good husband until you lose a few pounds."

"If this was a movie and the main character's mother said that no one would like you."

"But by the end of this movie, I bet that main character would have a man."

"Not because she stopped eating cookies!"

"We'll never know."

"Okay. Thanks for coming over, mom. I feel better. You can go."

Mom turned the sudoku book over, eyed the

chair beside her. I sat, still, occasionally, the obedient daughter. With a sigh so deep only a mother could reach, she said, "What are you going to do?"

"I've been writing again." Well, *thinking* about writing.

"Oh, Athena, let's be serious. I'll call Luanne. See if they are hiring."

"I'm not going to be a goddamned sales lady at Macy's, mother. I graduated from Northwestern."

"Well, even people who graduated from Northwestern need a job. How are you going to pay your rent?"

"Selling pictures of my feet on OnlyFans."

"Athena, you didn't!"

"I didn't... only because it appears I have ugly feet."

"ATHENA!"

"I'm kidding, mother." Sorta.

"Well..." Mother tried to smother her anxiety with a deep breath. "One great thing about Macy's, if you worked in the men's department..."

"Oh my god. You want me to work at a department store to find a husband. This isn't 1955!"

"If this was 1955, you'd be married with children."

"If this was 1955, I'd be a lesbian bartender in New York."

"I thought you were done with that phase."

"It wasn't a phase, mom. It was love."

"But you like men again? Chase was a man, right? You never even posted pictures of this one."

"Okay, time to go — go, go, go." I lifted her up by the elbow, marched her toward the door. As I tried to shove her out,

Mom spun toward me, gave me the hug I endured everything else for. "I love you so, so, so much, Athena."

"Love you, too, mom."

"Can I say one more thing?"

"Nope." Kissed her on the cheek, pushed her out, closed the door.

"'Meow," Ripper cried out as he emerged from his self-imposed isolation. My mother hated all cats so I told my black and orange tortie not to take it personally. He did anyway. Because even the feline males in my life lack perspective.

· · ·

Back in the kitchen, I peeled open the heroically rescued Oreos and ate my considerable feelings. Flipped through the sudoku book my mother had left behind.

Growing up, mom always had a book in hand. Almost always a mystery. And almost always Agatha Christie. To get her attention I had to do something more interesting than what was happening in her books. Which felt impossible. So by my junior year in high school, I decided to become a novelist. A mystery novelist. I'd be such a famous and respected writer, my mother would tell me, "You're more important to me than Agatha Christie."

Finished my first novel before I finished college.

(Okay, technically I finished *Confessions of a Teenage Broken Heart* in high school but that doesn't count for very dramatic reasons I'll explain later.)

Anyway, I found an agent shockingly easy and prepared for literary stardom. Except my agent dropped me when my first manuscript didn't sell. Wrote five more before I turned thirty. Three different agents couldn't sell any of them. My fifth agent gave me a generic best seller, said, 'Copy this. Copy the style. Copy the structure. Copy everything. Just change the names and the location. And I'll sell it. I promise.'

So my sixth book was *The Nanny*. About a, um, nanny for a rich suburban couple who witnesses a murder next door. And she sold it. For $43,000. Felt like a million. But I knew the book was terrible even if no one in the publishing industry did. The reviews were blandly positive. Felt like my agent had bribed every single one. When she asked me to write another one, 'but with more plot, less talking' after *The Nanny* had 95% less dialogue than my other five books, I fired her... and haven't written another word in three years.

Not long after that, I noticed my mom never read any more. Just did sudoku. When I asked her why, my mother said, "I don't think I ever liked books. I just like solving puzzles."

Sometime in the middle of the second row of Oreos, as panic started to creep in on how exactly I was going to pay rent and stave off the cruel demons feasting on my self worth, I got a text:

Athena. It's Elizabeth Diaz. Yes, that
one. I know we haven't talked since
all the drama but you remain the
most insightful person I've ever had
in my life. And I could really use the
famous 'Witchy West Wisdom'
right now.

I f I hadn't gotten fired that day for reading a book about a boy wearing a dress, if I hadn't gotten dumped over text by a man mad at me for being mad at him for cheating on me, I probably wouldn't have even texted Elizabeth back.

But I was in the perfect emotional state to make a terrible mistake.

Chapter Three

I was at O'Hare the next morning for a 7:55 AM Friday flight to Los Angeles. Didn't text mom where or why I was going (and that she'd need to feed Ripper) until the airplane doors closed. Then sent my phone to the mode designed to avoid judgements from your mother.

L ast night, after I texted Elizabeth back a meek but defiant *Hi*, she called before I could properly consider what I should do if she did.

"Hi, Elizabeth," I answered, burying all my nerves and rage with a voice usually saved for telemarketers.

"Athena! I'm so glad you answered. My text. My call. I miss you. Oh, my god, I miss you. I'm sorry. You know I'm sorry. I'm so sorry. But can that wait and can I make it up to you over the next fifty years?"

I managed only a, "Elizabeth," before she interrupted me with a thirty second recap of the sixteen years since we graduated high school. I pretended, rather well, that all of this was new information as if I hadn't been stalking her and Travis on social media the entire time. I tried another, "Elizabeth," only she interrupted me again, this time her voice in an escalating panic,

"Athena, can you come to San Evita? Come see me? Like soon? Maybe this weekend? I can buy your plane ticket and you'll have a room — a nice room, ocean view, and all the food you want."

"Elizabeth," I tried for the third time. When she didn't cut me off, I asked, "What is this about?"

"I'm in trouble." She dropped to a whisper, "I can't say too much on the phone. Oh, this is so weird. I know. I know you don't trust me. But I trust you and knowing I trust you can you trust me I wouldn't be asking if this wasn't maybe life or death important?"

"Where's San Evita?" I knew. But I had to ask so she wouldn't know I knew.

"It's north of L.A. Just south of Santa Barbara. It's the most beautiful place on earth. You'll love it. It will be a free vacation for you. I'm sure you'll tell me it's nothing. You'll tell me I'm being paranoid. But you always notice everything. If anyone can figure it out, it's you."

"Does this have to do with Travis?" I asked.

"No. Nooooo. I have to go. Please come? Text me when you can come and I'll have a ticket for you out of O'Hare."

She hung up. Anyone with any semblance of an actual life — a career, a spouse, a family, a dentist appointment — would have dismissed the incoherent cry for help from the woman who stole your first love *and* your first novel.

But only a special few like myself could have so little else going for us that the idea of being trapped at a resort with your ex-boyfriend and ex-best friend actually sounded like an escape from something far worse: irrelevance to the universe.

If only to make it impossible for my wiser self (or more likely my mother) to change my mind, I texted Elizabeth that I had a small window to visit but would need to come at once. Seven minutes later she texted me my flight information.

'''ve never been to Los Angeles. I had no idea there were palm trees inside the airport. I'm kidding. There aren't palm trees inside LAX but it *felt* like there were which is almost more shocking than actual palm trees.

Elizabeth had an Uber Black waiting for me. Texted it would be a two hour drive to San Evita. It took four. Listened to Taylor Swift the entire time. By the end of the ride felt fragile and invincible with equal ferocity. That's her super power.

I stepped out of the Expedition at just past four p.m. California time. Twenty-fours since being fired. And twenty-three hours and fifty-two minutes since being dumped.

No matter what the days ahead held, this was already the most event filled week since... well, since I discovered Elizabeth and Travis were sleeping together sixteen years ago.

Chapter Four

THE DESMOND DIAMOND Resort had originally been built by the Hollywood Studios to hide silver screen stars away for any condition that would tarnish their box office appeal. Substance abuse. Mental breakdowns. Pregnancies. Political inconveniences. It was located in its own narrow valley inside the Santa Ynez Mountains. Designed by an acolyte of Frank Lloyd Wright, the natural wood and cement hotel remained an architectural delight 72 years after being built. The u-shaped structure held eighty rooms, four boutiques, two restaurants, one spa, and a giant curved shaped pool with uninterrupted views down the valley, over the Pacific Coast highway, and deep into the ocean. A miniature golf course, eight tennis courts, eleven cabins, and miles of hiking trails filled the rest of the valley.

All this I stole off wikipedia. Including, *"And after years of neglect, Elizabeth and Travis Diaz, authors of the book which the Netflix series 'Confessions of a Teenage Broken Heart' was based on, bought the resort in hopes of restoring it to its former glory."*

But seeing the Desmond Diamond — *smelling it* — for the first time made my head light, stomach ache, and heart wonder. It also made me wish I had valued being rich over everything else, including love and happiness. Because I hadn't found either of those despite an unrelenting lifelong search for both. This might be hard for some of you youngsters to hear, but it's better to be alone, sad, and rich than alone, sad, and poor.

"Ms. West?" A feminine voice spun me away from my life-do-over daydreams and back to the reality that I was here for a reason not yet known.

"That's meeeeee."

"I'm Lilith Lennon, Ms. Diaz's assistant." She held out her hand. With the irrational sense I was agreeing to something unsavory, I shook it.

· · ·

Lilith Lennon was about my 5'7" but her obscenely aggressive heels left her towering over me. Something she enjoyed with explicit relish. She wore a coral business suit, a skirt long enough to sell seriousness and short enough to sell a good time. The jacket was buttoned high and tight, much to the dismay of a very proud pair of boobs. She was half asian, half white, and wholly stunning. Dark brown hair framed her face in such a way that her giant brown eyes devoured your own. Yet the most intimidating aspect of Lilith was she could only be 22 or 23 years old yet held herself — and my hand — as if she was ten years wiser than me. Her only blemish were pock mocks from teenage acne struggles that not even her elite make-up skills could hide.

"How was the trip in?" Lilith asked.

"Great," I said because neither of us wanted another answer.

"Ms. Diaz is busy right now with some very special guests. I wish I could tell you who, but part of the burden of working here is that you cannot boast about all the famous and important people you meet."

And yet she managed just that two sentences in. "You can just plop me in the lobby. I have a book I can read."

"Are you trying to get me fired, Athena?" She laughed as if I was a silly man who had made a bad joke.

"Should I be trying to get you fired?" I laughed back as if in on the joke. But seriously, Elizabeth should terminate this Lilith Lennon at once. She's clearly after everyone's job and everyone's husband and had the eyes, body, and personality to pull it off.

Lilith stopped laughing once she realized she didn't understand why I was. "Let me take you to your room. Can I help you with your luggage?" She reached for my grocery bag sized roller.

"I can manage."

The lobby's atrium stretched all four stories upward, capped by skylights that made it just as bright inside the hotel as it was outside. White oak floors, furniture pieces that each cost more than my annual teacher's salary, and the soothing ripple of an indoor waterfall. There were only four other guests in the lobby, but each was dressed as if preparing for a magazine cover shoot. All of this completed my best — and most devastating — vision of the life Elizabeth and Travis Diaz lived together here in iconic coastal California.

Followed Lilith to a glass elevator, once the doors closed us inside, she whispered, "Elizabeth wanted you to have an ocean view. Not the suites or the third floor — those start at two thousand dollars a night — but I picked you out my favorite on the second floor. Next to the stairs in case you need to make an emergency escape."

"Do you foresee me needing to make an emergency escape?" I asked, not in a whisper as I was pretty sure we weren't discussing military secrets.

"I'm a woman that likes to plan big entrances and quiet exits."

"I see." That line was too exquisite. If she came up with it on her own, in this moment, I should truly never attempt to write again. If she stole it, more likely and my favored scenario, then I was doubling down on the odds that Lilith Lennon was the villain in whatever story Elizabeth had written me into.

• • •

As we exited the elevator, Lilith pointed to Room 227 before opening it. Before I followed her in, I took one last look over the interior balcony down toward the lobby. I didn't know why I looked until I saw him.

Him.

Travis.

Traaaaaaavis.

Have you ever seen a sunset or painting or poem or puppy or child so beautiful that you can't believe something that beautiful exists and then you hate that something that beautiful exists because it reminds you so little else can be that beautiful and you know the emptiness in your heart once that beauty disappears from your life will never be filled for the rest of eternity?

So.

Yeah.

That's a lot of unresolved emotional trauma... but it's also what it was like seeing Travis Diaz for the first time in sixteen years from one floor up and one hundred meters away.

That he was talking or flirting or arguing with

someone I couldn't quite see only made it worse. I wanted that beautiful poem of a man to be yelling at me for any reason at all. Then I wanted to kiss him and then I wanted to murder him. My instinct to run around the 2nd floor until I was directly above him and then leap off the balcony on top of his head was held in check only by,

Lilith saying, "That's Travis Diaz. He's the co-owner of the hotel and Elizabeth's husband."

"Oh." I said this because I couldn't say, *He was my first boyfriend and first love and he cheated on me with my best friend and I have not trusted a man, woman, or feeling since.*

Travis and the faceless person (a woman? Probably.) disappeared down the south hall. Once he was out of sight, I felt the relief of being able to breathe again... followed at once by the desperate desire to find him again so I could *again* not breathe and then finally — mercifully — die.

"M s. West, are you okay?" Lilith asked. I turned. When the probable bad guy was feeling sorry for you, re-evaluations of your entire life should be scheduled.

"Yeeeeeeep."

Lilith didn't buy it but I didn't have the energy to re-sell it. Instead, I grabbed the keycard from her and let myself into room 227.

Bright whites and soft browns. A bed and television big enough to steal your time and concerns. The bathroom was larger than my apartment bedroom. The shower larger than my car. But all these niceties could be nice anywhere. The sliding doors at the end led to a wide balcony and that balcony led to an epic ocean view that was — at least for a few days — mine alone.

Lilith yet again interrupted my alternate universe fantasies with, "Elizabeth said you were here as an advisor on some hotel matters. No one here at the Desmond knows more about the hotel than me. I'd be happy to help you prepare for your meeting with Elizabeth by discussing the issues that brought you to us."

This was a bunch of very friendly sounding mish-mush that translated to, *Elizabeth hasn't told me why you're here and that's driving me insane.* To this I said, "That's incredibly kind of you. But I'd love to rest now and take you up on that offer after I first meet with Elizabeth."

Lilith's face contorted in protest. But I had already walked past her and opened the room door.

"Thanks again for welcoming me here, Lilith." She managed a half thought nod then slinked out, only to spin back with relish when I said, "Before you go... who was Mr. Diaz speaking with down in the lobby?"

She hated my question. "I did not recognize her," Lilith lied. Did she lie because there was something to hide or did she lie because she wanted to punish me for something else?

She laced her smile with silent curse words and walked off.

Saturday Morning

COFFEE
WITH
DETECTIVE BLUE

6:22 AM

Chapter Five

"Ms. West," Detective Blue interrupted. "I'll ask again. How did you 'sorta' murder Elizabeth Diaz?"

"I'm getting to that."

"You haven't been getting anywhere near that. You are wasting my time with excessive details about your trip to San Evita."

"I'm offering you important context on your other suspects... like Lilith Lennon."

"Lilith Lennon has an alibi at the time of death," Detective Blue mumbled. "So you can cease trying to implicate her."

"But you don't like her alibi."

"I didn't say that."

"Your eyes said it."

"Oh, boy. Fine. Continue with your excessive details of your visit. Just leave out the commentary."

"My commentary has all the insights and flair. You don't want just boring facts."

"That's exactly what I want."

"Your eyes say otherwise."

"Ms. West, I don't want commentary about what you think my eyes are saying either."

"And yet your eyes are saying they *do* want that."

"*Ms. West.*"

"Ugh. Fine. Just tell me how Lilith alibi'd out and I'll continue."

"No."

"She claimed she was with one of the other suspects, didn't she?"

Blue said nothing. But his eyes screamed.

Friday Afternoon

at the
Desmond
Diamond
Hotel

4:57 PM

Chapter Six

AFTER DEBATING whether I should wander the hotel grounds with equal hope and terror of running into Travis, my self-respect insisted that hadn't worked when I was eighteen and would be exponentially more pathetic at thirty-four.

Instead I opened the slider, let in the sea breeze and setting sunlight, then turned the bed toward the ocean. A thirteen minute pull and push, inch by inch. Surely not the first to do this but I'd like to think I now belong to a rare and special group.

Once lying down, did the shallowest of internet dives on Lilith Lennon. This wasn't unusual. My fascination with certain people can often slip onto the darker side of obsession. Always briefly. Except with Travis and Elizabeth.

Once my curiosity was quenched, I snuggled under the comforter. My anxiety wanted to replay all my terrible life choices, but the view and air said I deserved the deepest of sleeps only vacation naps can provide.

A violent knock at my hotel room that could re-animate the dead launched me off the bed and face first to the floor. "Coming!" I yelled, crawling on hands and knees as if this was the most efficient means of travel. Half way there, I officially realized I was One, awake and Two, needed to stand. Once at the door, I peeked through the eyehole to find a young man on the other side. He was just generically attractive enough that I almost opened the door without first making sure he wasn't a serial killer. Instead I yelled as if not a foot away from him, "Who is it?"

"It's Derek Shapiro, the Assistant Manager."

Decided those words were the password and swung open the door. "Hiiiiii," I said and noted to myself that I really must work on not extending vowels.

"Ms. Diaz said you were not answering your

phone and that I should retrieve you for your dinner."

I twisted back toward the bed only to notice the black of night had fallen on my view. "What time is it?"

Derek glanced at his watch. "8:12."

"I napped for three hours," I said aloud as if to make it real.

"Congratulations. I work twelve hours a day, seven days a week and haven't had a nap since I was twenty-three."

"I'm impressed." I was not, but he needed to hear that I was. "How old are you now, Derek?"

"Twenty-six. I went to Cornell."

"That's amazing," and by amazing I mean it was amazing it took him less than one minute to let me know he went to an Ivy League school.

"What would be amazing is if I could get you to Angelico's for your dinner with Ms. Diaz."

"I'll need to shower and change."

"That's not necessary."

"And yet it is."

"I'm very busy. I cannot simply wait here while you get ready."

"Nor should you. I'll find my way to the restaurant."

"But — "

"Thanks, Derek," and I let the door shut. In his face.

While every twenty-something woman I classify as either my competition or my protege, every man in their twenties I can't help but think of as teenagers pretending to be adults. Their aspirations remain focused on two things: taking over the world or convincing a woman to assist with an orgasm. And since all fail at the first, getting off takes on the stakes of taking over the world. Which means, for these teenage-twenty-something males, every sexual encounter feels existentially important in the moment and an utter disappointment afterwards.

Derek Shapiro, noted graduate of Cornell University, with his bright teeth that he knew never to cover with lips, a dark blue suit tight enough to let his biceps boast, and confidence that could not contain his cockiness, was convinced both of his destiny to rule the world and his privilege to rule over any woman.

. . .

After showering, I put on black Lululemon stretch trousers that for $140 made my soft legs look athletic and my butt appear as firm as a cookie-loving soul could hope for. I wore a light purple sweater, loose at my "couple extra pounds" waist and tight over my "couple extra pounds" chest. Naked ankles, bright white Converse Chucks. My hair, after much internal debate, was put into a pony-tail because my hair was the President of the "Athena must not ever grow up" club.

No matter how big my ego grew (in the year after college when I assumed fame and fortune were days away) or low my self-esteem dropped (after every book and lover rejection since), I knew I could present myself to both friends and suitors alike as attractive yet approachable, smart yet silly, the girl next door... who knew how to talk dirty when the time was right. The biggest downside to my presentation was time had proved it great at attracting the cool, hungry vampires and awful at finding me people who didn't want to suck the life out of me.

· · ·

When I opened my hotel room door, Derek was waiting there. "You're still here," I said with unfiltered astonishment.

"I had failed to express the value I might have in escorting you down to dinner."

I stepped past him and to the elevator. "Ah. This is true. You're the Assistant Manager here, correct?"

"I am. And no one — not even Elizabeth — knows more about the Desmond Diamond than I."

"Lilith Lennon, the assistant to the manager, and the second half of your Dwight Schrute, said the same." Derek trailed me into the elevator as it opened.

"I don't follow your popular television references — " Yet he did. "— but Lilith has been here less than eight months — "

"And you've been here — "

"Almost two years."

"While Elizabeth *bought* the resort four years ago, correct?"

"Yes, but — and I don't mean to dismiss Elizabeth's extensive knowledge — "

"And yet you already have." Usually said things

like that only in my head. Some men required bluntness I suppose.

As we landed on the first floor, Derek pressed the elevator doors closed and stepped between me and the exit.

A small voice in my head reminded me that my flippancy about my mortality did not actually make me immortal... and that creepy, entitled men like Derek were responsible for far too many violent crimes against women. He pressed his girth against me until I stepped back, whispered with equal menace and desperation, "Ms. West, I only mean to say that Elizabeth has to spend much of her time dealing with the broader aspects of running the hotel and it falls to me to be on top of every detail. You would be wise to tell me why you're truly here." The last sentence a naked threat.

The voice that cared whether I lived or died at the hands of someone like Derek failed to stop my inner tough bitch from shoving him to the side with one hand. He didn't like a woman moving him out of the way. His eyes wanted to hurt me. But his breath sped, his shoulders shrunk because deep down he was afraid of a woman that could push back.

I said as the elevator opened, "Well, I don't know who knows more between you and Lilith. I do know both of you like to whisper in closed elevators. And I've decided, at this exact second, I don't trust people who whisper in closed elevators." I stepped brashly past him, very proud of my *loud* elevator speech. As I strutted toward the restaurant,

Derek called out, "Ms. West..."

I turned back if only to confirm my triumph.

"The restaurant is the other direction."

He grinned with enough smugness it might cause a worldwide shortage. For the moment, my only comeback was to google his ass for information ammunition I'd probably need by our next encounter.

Chapter Seven

ANGELICO'S WAS in the southwest corner of the hotel, down one of the 'U' halls, past tiny, shiny shops filled with clothes I couldn't afford and I'd never wear yet I yearned for as if they'd give life meaning.

I slowed when passing the Nirvana Spa. The lights were off. Door closed. But standing deep inside the shadows was Lilith, having an animated conversation with a young woman. This young woman had blonde hair pulled back in a pony-tail. Naturally pretty, naturally curvy, unnaturally afraid of Lilith.

I avoid most avoidable conflict but bullies are a trigger and Lilith yelling at this young woman had triggered that trigger. Heightening my mother hen response was that this young woman looked eerily like the daughter I always thought I'd have and was only now realizing I probably never would.

So I smacked my hand hard against the store window, jolting Lilith my way. Waved as if I was just saying hello. Lilith faked a fake smile then joined me in the hall.

"Good evening, Ms. West. How's your stay so far?" But Lilith was far more concerned about the young woman in the spa emerging than how my hotel experience was unfolding.

"Took a three hour nap," I said because this remained my biggest accomplishment in years.

"Research shows that naps are one of the best ways to improve your health and extend your life. I'm just too young to prioritize such things over the demands of my job."

"Ha. Yes. Maybe you are."

She leaned close. Her familiar whisper hissed, "I assume you're on your way to meet Elizabeth for dinner. Just remember the best way to get away with murder is to choose the detective assigned to the case." *Again* a line I admired too much not to be suspicious of its origins.

"Are you planning to murder someone, Lilith?"

"It's a metaphor."

"Oh. I see. Perhaps I'm too old to understand it."

"Yes, perhaps. Good luck, Ms. West." Lilith slithered off toward the lobby.

One foot of mine tried to walk on towards my dinner with Elizabeth but my other three limbs insisted I duck into the Nirvana Spa and check on my young doppelgänger. She turned toward me, attempting to hide her tear filled face with a brave smile. Had come to California to wrestle demons from my past not rescue daughters from alternate universes yet I could not stop myself from saying,

"You okay?"

"Me? Oh. Yes. Sorry. I'm fine." In the history of the English language, no phrase has ever meant the opposite of its face definition more than *I'm fine.*

Four years ago, just after turning thirty, I was driving home past midnight after sleeping with a man that One, I was not attracted to, Two, I knew would be bad in bed, and Three, I'd never see again because he was both boring and mean. On this drive of shame, as tears poured and Taylor cried out my soul's anguish, a cat ran out in front of my Mini. I screamed, sure I had run it over. But then I looked in the rearview mirror and saw him huddled in the middle of the road. Slammed on the breaks, jumped out, sprinted back along the center line, waving my hands with a madness that hoped the cat would survive. Or I'd die. At that moment, either would have been a win.

The cat didn't move. My craziness can occasionally inspire paralysis. I scooped him up, drove straight to a 24-hour vet, and named him Ripper after Jack because I was in that kind of a mood.

This is all meant to illustrate that I do have a history of taking in strays.

"I'm Athena," I said to the young woman with eyes she could have stolen from me.

"Diana..." she said, the deepness of her voice contrasting with the fragility of her face.

"I'm a stranger in a strange hotel, but I'm also old enough to have shed too many tears for too many different reasons not to recognize someone who could use a sympathetic ear."

After a moment to process my offer, Diana

nodded with apprehension that soon blossomed into enthusiasm.

"So," I started, "are we crying over work? Love? Both?"

"I think it's both."

"Been there. So not only is your heart broken, but now your job feels emotionally unsafe. Is it someone at the spa?" I pointed to her uniform.

"Oh?" Diana glanced down, as if forgetting what she was wearing. "No... this job... is just a job... I'm a writer..."

"Oh?" Her being a writer made me want to cry for both of us.

"Yes, I know it's not a sensible career choice — "

"Your mom tell you that?"

"My dad."

"I find most writers have parents who never had the sense to first understand their children before lecturing them on what's sensible for them."

"Yes..." Diana said, "Yesssss!" Then it dawned on her, "You're a writer, too, aren't you?"

"I..." almost said 'sorta' but instead just said, "I am."

"You must be very successful to stay at a hotel like this. I bet you write for TV. What show? I bet I've watched it. I watch everything."

"Alas, I don't and I'm not. One published novel you won't have heard of."

"I bet I have. I read about every new published book."

"Mine came out five years ago — " Had it really been that long? Can I still call myself a writer?

"What's the title, please tell me, I might have even read it — "

"The Nanny," I said and braced for,

"Oh, mmmh, I don't..."

"It's okay. I wish I hadn't heard of my book either."

"I bet it's amazing," Diana insisted, but then transitioned to, "Did you know the owners of this hotel are Travis and Elizabeth Diaz? Maybe you don't know their names but they wrote the novel *Confessions of a Teenage Broken Heart* which is the novel that made me want to be a writer..."

So my daughter from another universe became a writer because of the book I wrote not too long after she was born?

. . .

"Diana," I started and I didn't know if I was going to tell a lie that felt true or confess a truth that would smell like a lie.

Her phone ringing saved me from choosing. "Hi," she answered. The short, loaded 'hi' could only be meant for the person that broke her heart. She listened, her face burning into a deep red working to contain lust or anger or, likely, both. Then, when she had heard enough from her former/future lover, she gagged on her own words of romantic submission, "Fine. I'm coming." After hanging up, her eyes avoided mine.

"It's okay," I said.

"What's okay?"

"To give them another chance or another night or whatever it is your heart is telling you to give."

"Even when you know they're gonna keep breaking that heart?"

"It's not okay for them to keep breaking your heart. But it's more than okay for you to keep hoping they won't."

"You're really wise."

"Just old."

"I'm going to read your book and then write you about how amazing it is."

"I'd like that. Hope your night has a happy ending, Diana."

"Yours, too, Athena." My doppelgänger ran off. Skipped even. Big hair. Thin legs. An old soul with young eyes. Irrational belief in her hopeful heart. I envied everything about Diana except the day she realized her heart had hoped its last hope.

Chapter Eight

IN THE OPPOSITE direction of disappearing Diana was an aged wood door which opened to a narrow hall which spilt into an old school Italian restaurant, complete with low ceilings, dim lighting, a long bar, and black-tied male waiters all born before 1969. At first glance they appeared to out number the restaurant patrons.

"You look like an Athena," a male voice said as he emerged from behind the bar.

"I aaaaaam." I have a problem.

"I'm Zai," he said.

· · ·

His long blonde hair had a bounce and shine that left my locks with an inferiority complex. His neck, arms, chest had natural thickness to them, earned by early morning ocean swims or wrestling bears under moonlight. His blue eyes neon beacons in this medieval establishment. His youth shocking compared to the ancient waiters. Yet he held a stillness that only a thousand year old wizard could possess.

(Shit. I'm attracted to this man. Don't say anything stupid.)

"Hi, Zaiiiiiiiii." Too late.

He smiled at me. As if I was a teenage girl with a crush. He squeezed my arm, spoke with a gentle firmness, "Elizabeth has a special table in the back. Follow me." Then he winked. Of course he did. I had always been immune to the appeal of younger men. 'Had' the operative word.

"Okaaaaaaaay."

The wait staff parted around him as if he was a battleship in a sea filled with row boats. I sailed behind him, not looking at his butt. And when I say I wasn't looking at his butt I really mean I was trying really hard not to look.

We twisted through tables, up steps, down steps, into another narrow hall. This one as dark as a rural highway. If Zai stopped, I'd be helpless but to run into him. He'd turn around to see if I was okay. I'd kiss him, pretending it was an accident if he didn't kiss me back. If he *did* kiss me back, I'd probably — no definitely — be having sex tonight. I'd get over a break-up in Athena-record time. I bet Zai has stamina. And I bet he could go for a second round. Maybe a third. When was the last time I was with a man who could have sex multiple times in one night? Years. Years and years. *Oh, Zai...*

"Yes, ma'am?" A voice said. *His voice.* He was standing, facing me. We were out of the dark hall, into a small room.

"Huh?"

"You said, 'Oh, Zai'."

"I did?"

"You did."

Mortification turned me to stone. If he touched me, I'd tip over, shatter into a million pieces. Honestly it would be a relief from his answering my accidental, aching, 'Oh, Zai' with a 'Yes, ma'am.'

All my pent-up sexual frustration and subsequent embarrassment vanished as Zai stepped aside to reveal a face I hadn't seen for sixteen years...

A face I used to love.

A face I used to hate.

A face that would be dead by Saturday morning.

57

PART TWO

THE LITTLE DEATHS AND THE LAST SUSPECT

Saturday Morning

COFFEE
WITH
DETECTIVE BLUE

6:39 AM

Chapter Nine

"SHE WAS dead by Saturday morning because of *you!*"
Blue yelled out, trying on a Mean Cop persona that
was so ill-fitting I had to stifle a smile. And my
snark. Verbally. My eyes held back nothing. Still, my
silence shamed Blue into: "Ms. West, sorry for my
outburst but I feel I have been very patient with your
drawn out confession."

"Detective Blue, I can only confess after we've
eliminated all other suspects." Drew a flower over
Zai's name.

"Ms. West, if you cannot take this more seriously
for your own sake then maybe you can do it for the
sake of Elizabeth."

"You're right — but can I first ask if Blue is really
your last name? Such an unusual last name."

"My mother was an actress — "

"Ooh. That explains a lot."

"What — HOW does that explain anything? Never mind. Why did you kill her, Ms. West?"

"I'm starting to feel like I'm your prime suspect."

"You're my *only* suspect."

"Detective Blue, my goodness, I'll accept being your prime suspect but your only one? Ignoring Travis and all the reasons the spouse is the first suspect on any list, there's Lilith Lennon, her questionable alibi, unchecked ambition and uncontrolled anger. Derek Shapiro, the Cornell educated assistant manager, and his disdain slash fear of powerful women? And lastly but certainly not leastly, I'll bet you dinner we both know why Zai would want to kill Elizabeth."

I'll often make silly bets with men I like. Usually bets that disguise my intentions for a first date. But Blue ignored my date trap and instead texted someone on his phone.

"Detective Blue, did I just give you reasonable doubt that I might not be your only suspect?"

"No," he lied but lied like he wanted me to know he was lying. I found this alluring. Yes, I know this isn't healthy.

But then panic gripped me that Blue might find

out more than I wanted, forcing me to ask, "Have you accounted for Zai's whereabouts at... wait, it just occurred to me that for Lilith to have alibi'd out, you must have determined the approximate time of death. I'd very much like to know this."

"*Ms. West*, you tell me when you killed her and I'll have the exact time of death."

"One a.m," I said.

Blue's face burst into fevered excitement. "The only way you could know that is if you killed Elizabeth."

"So it was one a.m.?"

"You just said it was!"

"I guessed. You confirmed." Blue's excitement faded as fast as it rose. I added, "I was hoping it was later." Crossed out one a.m. on my notepad. Then wrote it again, but in bubble letters. Then colored in the bubble letters.

I *needed to talk to Zai...*

. . .

Blue, reading my briefly desperate face, asked, "Why would you hope it was later —"

"I'll tell you later why I wish it was later. You sure about one a.m.? Because now I hate I guessed one a.m. But you sound sure. You don't have security cam footage of the murder or else this would all be a waste of time."

"There are no cameras by the cabins. But the security camera system inside the hotel wasn't working, Ms. West, because you sabotaged it."

"True. In addition to being an unemployed kindergarten teacher and unsuccessful novelist, I am also a world renowned security system saboteur."

"MS. WEST! YOU said YOU killed her. *That's* why you're my prime suspect."

"I said 'sorta'... so we should explore why I didn't say I *definitely* killed her before we can analyze why I said sorta."

His frustration, predictably, boiled over... but this was the type of frustration that overflows from a man's head down into his other one. I've never known a man — and I've known *too* many men — who didn't become sexually aroused once frustrated enough. And here's a confession I can make right now: a man turned on by his frustration with me *turned* me on. Yes, this was both a ridiculous and self-fulling cycle. But facts are facts. And turn ons are turn ons. "Detective Blue... do you have a first name?"

"No."

I smiled. I really wanted to kiss him now. Not just in spite of his mustache but because of it. "Do you have lunch plans?"

His frustration was exploding. So were my inappropriate thoughts. "Sorry. Didn't mean to ask you to lunch. Not yet anyway. Unless you'll say yes already?"

His eyes said no.

"That's fair. Okay. Let's dive into my dinner — and my tortured history with the one and only — "

Friday Night

at the
Desmond
Diamond
Hotel

8:36 PM

Chapter Ten

"*Elizabeth*," the word spilled from my mouth as if I didn't have room for it. She leapt from the small corner booth, flung her arms wide. Squeezed my torso with vigor, her mouth lunged at my ear as if to bite it. But instead,

Elizabeth whispered, "I can't believe you actually came."

"Me neither." Seriously.

"You're prettier than me now," Elizabeth said as she pulled out of our embrace.

"Impossible," I said. She had been voted Homecoming Queen and Most Likely to win an Oscar. But maybe she was sorta right? I mean, Elizabeth was still thinner than me (of course she was) and her make-up was flawless and she dressed like the boss that she was. But the years of stress and sun had weathered and leathered her skin. And though it was unprovable I'd also like to think the guilt of her betrayal had slowly vacuumed the pretty from her year after year, pore by pore. (I also have one of those faces that was considered plain when I was kid but then slowly evolved from 'not bad' to 'sorta cute' to 'almost pretty' to 'maybe beautiful' as I neared thirty-five. I'm gonna be a really hot senior citizen.)

Elizabeth said, "Liar. Come sit. Let's eat carbs like we're sixteen years old and tell each other everything."

Zai lingered as we slipped into the round booth. He spoke with a sudden self-conscious awkward-ness, "Ms. Diaz, I'll have Little Dave work the bar as it would be an honor to wait upon you two gorgeous ladies this evening."

Elizabeth eyes fired bullets through his forehead. "No, Zai. Didn't need you to walk Athena back here. Don't need you to wait on us. I need you behind the bar. Send Pietro or Dominque."

Drooping like a scolded puppy, Zai mumbled, "Yes, Ms. Diaz," then slunk off into the dark hall.

Once we were alone, Elizabeth said, "Some

employees let their eagerness get the best of them. Hard lesson to learn."

"I bet," I said but here's the thing I didn't say: Elizabeth was sleeping with him.

I was a good but not great kindergarten teacher.

I was a determined but not brilliant mystery novelist.

I was a talented but not ground breaking lover. (I giggled at any discussion or requests or actual touching of butt stuff.)

But there was one skill that, if it were an Olympic sport, I'd be world champion: I could always tell when two people were fucking.

Unfortunately this ability had no monetary value. I'm not sure it had any non-monetary value either. I suppose it helped with a few dramatic plot twists in my books. But mostly it had helped me know when a boyfriend was cheating on me. The first being Travis... with Elizabeth.

. . .

ut on this night in San Evita, California, I did not bring up the past. Nor her affair with Zai. (Oh, sweet Zai, you betrayed me before I even met you.) Instead I spent the first hour with Elizabeth recapping my life since high school as if it was a raunchy sex comedy and not a tragic lifetime of heartbreak. (I can be quite funny. If this is the first you're picking up on this, I've failed in my own character development completely.)

Only after lusciously buttered bread rolls, heavy caesar salads and heavier pink sauce over lobster ravioli did I finally turn the night to the reason for this re-union:

"So, Elizabeth. Why. Am. I. Here?"

She glanced toward the hall to make sure no one was coming. Then out the window toward the ocean in case the whales were gossips. When she re-focused on me, a gravity had fallen over her tiny emerald eyes. The gravity was heavier than the pink sauce. So heavy, I dare say, it might be performative: "Athena… I have no proof but deep in my heart I can't help but believe that Travis is cheating on me."

"Oh, that's terrible," I said. My performance lacked Elizabeth's motivation.

"Liar… you're thinking this is karma."

"Noooooo." I was thinking this was something

else entirely.

Years Ago

Nineteen and a Half Years Ago
(To Be Slightly More Precise)

Chapter Eleven

NINETEEN DAYS after freshman year started, Elizabeth Hudson walked into first period A.P. biology. I was the only one without a partner because I was the only one in class without a friend. She wore tight black jeans, a dark red sweater, and black boots with heels I couldn't balance on today let alone at fourteen. I hated her long eyelashes and her runway walk and how she knew all the boys were staring at her but she pretended they didn't exist... I hated it so much *and* wanted her to teach me all of it.

Elizabeth had moved from New York. Not just New York. *Manhattan.* Something she reminded me every time something about suburban Riverbend, Illinois, felt, well, suburban. Her father had an affair — the common trauma that bonded us so profoundly — and her mom pulled Elizabeth and her sister from their private school, personal chef, limitless credit card life and dragged them to live with cousins they barely knew.

As thankful as I was that Elizabeth had been seated next to me on her first day, I held no illusions that the more popular girls with their access to parties, boys, and social ladders would be her final destination.

Yet she never left my side.

Eventually I asked why she stuck with the nerdy girl in the 'Hermione For President' hoodies (note this was pre-problematic Rowling) and she said something generic like I was smart and funny. But my gut said, after her parent's ugly divorce, Elizabeth saw in me a person who would never betray her, never abandon her. And yes, sorta, because of my qualities like honesty and loyalty, but also because my socially undesirable traits would ensure I'd never have a better option to leave her for.

It says a lot about my (in)ability to make friends that by the 4th day of Elizabeth's arrival from New York, she was my best friend. Not just new best friend but best friend I'd ever had and — and this is so brutal to confess — the best friend I've had since.

She re-organized her schedule to get all the

same classes with me. We joined the same clubs (yes, the Quidditch club, but also the fashion club even as I clung to my baggy sweatshirts). And we talked for hours on the phone every night despite having just spent the entire day together.

By Christmas I confessed to my mother I was in love with Elizabeth. She said it wasn't love. I cried out, "But I love everything about her and want to spend every minute with her!" She cooly insisted, "If you tell Elizabeth you love her she will think you're weird and never speak to you again." This remains the worst thing my mother has ever said to me. (And she's said a lot of terrible things.) Sometimes I'd imagine an alternate timeline where I did confess I loved her and Elizabeth said she loved me back and Travis Diaz never entered either of our lives and... alas...

Anyway. Never told Elizabeth I felt anything more than 'I love you so, so, so much as a friend' and we flew through freshman year and most of sophomore year as only soul mates can fly through time. But then Elizabeth started talking about boys. And so I talked about boys mostly because I wanted to talk about everything with her.

· · ·

Elizabeth liked to daydream about every cool/hot boy at school. If she let her eyes linger on any of them for more than thirty seconds, they'd dare to approach her at lunch only for her to shoo them away as morons for thinking she wanted to talk to them.

Me? I had a single crush: Nathaniel Kelly, the type of boy who read the *Game of Thrones* books long before the HBO series aired. He was short, glasses thicker than mine, but had Ronald Weasly's red hair which was my first romantic kryptonite. When I first discussed him with Elizabeth, I had no feelings for Nathaniel just a very faint 'hey, he's not totally unappealing'. But over the next six months as Elizabeth discussed fifty different boys, I only talked about Nathaniel and at some point I must have convinced myself I was in love with him and would die if he didn't like me back. So I asked Nathaniel to the sophomore Turnabout dance. His response: *"Unfortunately I have a rule that I can only date women with a higher GPA than me."* He was ranked first in our class.

His rejection sent me into my first (of far too many) broken hearted spirals. My mother had, according to legend, gotten over her divorce during a single Jazzercize class. Thus she had neither the patience nor the experience to comprehend the depths of my despair. Elizabeth tried but her disgust at my being upset over the 'boy with all the freckles' was the first tear in our friend-love. So I opened up the diary I hadn't cracked since 4th grade.

In it I poured.

Much of it indulgent ramblings of a 15 year-old girl who didn't know enough about love to know I didn't know anything about love. But the magic in the madness was a poem entitled, *Dreams Die After Dinner*. The first time I re-read it, I knew it was great. To this day, still might be the greatest thing I've written. It was so great a voice inside me demanded it be shared. I told the voice absolutely not. That voice tied up the Athena that was mortified of sharing anything, even her bare ankles, and locked her in the closet.

For years it would turn out.

As fate would have it the next day were the auditions for the school's variety show. I strutted onto stage, bellowed my poem, and strutted off. The power I felt that moment — power drawn from the evolutionary leap destiny had demanded of me — was a feeling I had been chasing ever since.

My poem's performance made the variety show. The director put me in black leggings and a black turtleneck. It made sense. It captured the darkness of my piece. But it was also tight. The dorky girl hiding behind oversized clothes and glasses was suddenly the girl with the words of fire and curves to match.

Elizabeth said she loved this new Athena. But really she hated her. Didn't know it then, but I was maturing into someone who would have options. And that terrified her. If we had enough time to work through this new friendship phase without anyone distracting us we might have emerged stronger than ever.

But Travis Diaz pounced. We didn't have a chance.

Friday Night

at the
Desmond
Diamond
Hotel

9:21 PM

Chapter Twelve

"So, Elizabeth," I said to the 34 year-old stranger with the name of my high school best friend, "when you said this had nothing to do with Travis it actually has *everything to do with Travis.*"

"Would you have come out if you knew it was about Travis?"

"No," I said but probably meant yes. "Why do you think I'm the one to help with this?"

"Because you see things no one else sees."

"Discovering you and Travis were sleeping with each other behind my back did not require any super powers, Elizabeth."

"I read your blog, Athena. Every post. You see shit no one else does years before most even think to start looking."

"My blog…" An experiment in publicly displayed stream of consciousness. Mercifully put out to pasture a few days after my thirtieth birthday.

Elizabeth said, "I've cyberstalked you since the day you stopped talking to me."

"I've stalked you, too."

Elizabeth reached across the table and took my hands in hers. "I love you, Athena."

"I love you, too, Elizabeth…" Wow.

"…as a friend."

"Huh?"

"You always added 'as a friend.'"

"I did?" Thanks Mom.

She smiled. She knew. Squeezed her hands as if to say 'I'm sorry'. My heart tried to re-write the past sixteen years into a happy ending for Elizabeth Holden and Athena West.

But my heart was a slow writer and before I could get through page one, Derek plowed into the room.

Elizabeth dropped my hands as if she never held them, said, "The bachelorette party in 404?"

"The bachelorette party in 404," Derek confirmed.

Elizabeth turned to me. The warmth in her eyes now cold. "I have to deal with this."

Odd the hotel owner was also the manager. Odder still she'd have to put out every small fire. But it was not the time or my place.

As she stood up Elizabeth said, "Can I check in later?"

"Yes. I'll just wait in my room."

Elizabeth leaned on the table, looming over me. "Or you could go find him. Use that Witchy West Wisdom to uncover all the secrets I'm too blind too see."

Sensed something behind her eyes. Had to ask, "Has Travis hurt you physically?"

"Noooo... no, no... You know Travis..." This was a loaded denial.

"I *knew* him."

"Just find out who he's sleeping with, Athena. That will answer everything else." So there was *something* else besides this supposed affair.

As Elizabeth spun to leave, I had to finally ask, "Why..."

She stopped, but didn't turn to face me.

Braved the question I had yearned to ask for half my life, "Why'd you sleep with him, Elizabeth... and why did you put your name on my book?"

Without turning, she said, "Maybe that's the

real mystery, Athena," then followed Derek into the hall.

It was the last time I saw Elizabeth Diaz alive.

Saturday Morning

COFFEE
WITH
DETECTIVE BLUE

6:54 AM

Chapter Thirteen

STOPPED my tale for the first time without a Detective Blue interruption. I offered the blandest of observations, "You're quiet."

He peeled back a brown folder, shoving a picture of Elizabeth's dead body to the tip of my nose. She was lying face down on the steps to the mountain-side cabin behind the hotel. Her hand outstretched toward the door. A circle of blood pooled in the small of her back. *Stabbed in the back.* How many times had I accused her of that in those angry college letters?

I asked, "She was killed with a kitchen knife?"

"You tell me, Ms. West."

"Odds are yes. There's Angelico's and the Ocean cafe. Any other kitchens? Room service have their own kitchen? Probably not. Do Angelico's and the cafe use the same cutlery?" Drew a knife through one of my flowers. Then a few notes just in case I got distracted later.

Blue's frustration deflated into boredom. Not good.

"You don't have the murder weapon, do you?" I asked with a coolness that woke Blue back up.

"It's where you hid it. We know it must be on the resort grounds. We'll find it eventually but if you want to let us know where it is now I'd appreciate saving my team the leg work."

"Well, I'd be a pretty boring suspect if I just told you where I hid the murder weapon. You expect more of me, Detective Blue." I winked. It felt earned.

"Your friend is dead and you are displaying no signs of sadness which, from my experience, is usually a sign of guilt."

"Oh. I see. You're a linear thinker. That's okay. Most people are. Linear people make sure the world keeps spinning."

"And what are you?" His frustration contorted into confusion.

"A non-linear thinker."

"And *what* does that mean?"

"It means that I've fantasized so many times

about Elizabeth's death for the past sixteen years — and experienced all the sadness and elation at such an event — that the reality of it cannot produce any more emotions than the ones I felt every time I imagined it." This sounded more true than it was.

"So you've been fantasizing about killing Elizabeth Diaz for sixteen years?"

"I..." was thinking that Blue's skin looked very soft. Very cuddle-able. I'd make him lay that supple cheek on the top of my head every time we watched *Murder She Wrote*. (Don't mock that show until you know what I know.)

"Ms. West, what are you thinking about that's more important than the murder of your best friend?"

"I..." began again but of course I couldn't tell him I was thinking about us Netflix-ing-and-chilling so I said, "I think it's time for that coffee."

"What coffee?"

"One of the uniformed officers asked if I wanted coffee when he dragged me out of my room at 4 am. I said not yet. I said I had to first wake up enough to know this wasn't a dream before I'd be ready for coffee." Blue's frustration leveled up beyond adorable to lovable. Was I falling in love with Detective Blue? Alas, I knew far too much about love to actually believe that.

"Fine," he mumbled. "Fine, fine… I'll get you a coffee."

"A mocha-vanilla latte with oat milk. An extra shot only if the large comes with just three. Hopefully the sweetener is powder in which case it's an easy half scoop of each. If it's liquid, I have very specific pump instructions that I'll write down."

"I'll get you a cup of black coffee and pretend you never said whatever the hell you just said."

"Blue, baby…"

His face froze in shocked shock.

"Sorry. Without my morning coffee and sugar I get… familiar…"

"What time did Elizabeth leave you in the restaurant's private room?"

"A little before ten."

"And you said you went back to your room after that?"

"I never said that."

"You — "

"I told Elizabeth I'd wait there but then she said I should go find Travis…"

"And so you went and found Travis?"

I held my ground.

"Ms. West, what happened after you left Angelico's?"

Hooooold.

"Ms. West!"

Hooooooooold.

"Fine. Dammit. I'll go get your goddamn latte."

lue left the room. Yes, my abandonment issues kicked in even when the person leaving was a cop convinced I was a murderer...

But I did need my latte.

Almost as much as I needed to get my stories straight before I confessed to more than I wanted him to know.

See, I had begun to think Detective Blue might be my soul mate. I know, I know. This is insane. He thinks I murdered Elizabeth. Worse, he might be right. But I have a theory —

(I have a lot of theories.)

— that not just under-loved, under-sexed, over-romantic spirts like myself have involuntary daydreams about total strangers being their future spouses or lovers or, yes, soul mates. I'm convinced even my mother has these thoughts despite no proof she has gone on a single date in twenty five years.

My point is that I needed to have a clear plan and a clearer head. So more notes were written. Then more flowers drawn. Then notes. Flowers. Notes. Flowers. And so on.

By the time Detective Blue returned nineteen minutes later, I had devised a more than competent (maybe even sorta brilliant) strategy to tell him just enough he might fall in love with me in that 1% chance he was my soul mate... but not so much he could arrest me for murder.

Friday Night

at the
Desmond
Diamond
Hotel

9:48 PM

Chapter Fourteen

After Elizabeth followed her assistant manager Derek Shapiro out of the room, I sat alone in the booth contemplating why Elizabeth really had brought me to the Desmond Diamond Hotel.

Travis may be having an affair. But Elizabeth's dalliance with Zai made it unlikely that marital infidelity alone held the consequences she alluded to over the phone.

Unconsciously did a Trivago search for a Desmond fourth floor suite price. $479.89 for tomorrow night. A Saturday in March. Not nothing. But not the two thousand a night Lilith spoke of. My eyes had already registered a lobby empty of guests, stores empty of customers, and a restaurant empty of patrons.

My amateur level internet sleuthing had never offered me precise numbers of what Travis and Elizabeth got paid for *Confessions of a Teenage Broken Heart*. My most paranoid fears said north of ten figures. But Travis's overeagerness for fame and relevance might have left them with far less even if Elizabeth's cooler head protected them from being completely ripped off.

Buying this hotel would have been Elizabeth's rational decision. But maybe her own eagerness for a famous real estate trophy to show off to her aloof and absent father led her to pay too much or take on too much debt.

Without an unfiltered look into their bookkeeping — and an accountant to interpret it for me — all this was just a guess. But my gut said this guess was far more relevant to the core of Travis and Elizabeth's troubles than any affairs by either of them.

T he only way I'd uncover the deeper truth of why my ex-best friend lured me out to California would be to find her husband. Which means I'd have to find myself in the same room with Travis Diaz. *A man so exquisite I wanted to possess him and then kill him.*

Which I dreaded.

And which was also the true reason I had *let* myself be lured here.

So I stood from my safe corner booth in my safe private dining room and weaved my way out from the depths of Angelico's...

...only to be intercepted at the host stand by the singular Zai.

(If I wrote romance novels, I'd want him on the cover. I might write a romance novel if only to ask him to pose for it.)

"Athena..." His soft voice sung, sorta, as he spread his legs to lower to my height.

"Hi, Zai." Didn't extend my vowels. Progress. He took my arm in his hands and — before I could comprehend why — started writing numbers with a black sharpie on the underside of my wrist.

"I want you to have my number. You are all alone here. Maybe you need someone to have lunch with... maybe you need someone to have breakfast with." His eyes sparkled to sell his inference. *I got it,*

Zai. Trust me. Most men are books with more pictures than words.

"That's sweet of you," and it would have been *really* sweet if he wasn't already sleeping with the one person I refused to take the sloppy seconds of.

"Plus, I know how much you care about Elizabeth — and I care about Elizabeth so much too — and I would love your help, or maybe you help me, who knows, in helping her. She's going through a very rough time..."

"I had no idea..." I said and tried to sell naiveté to someone with a lifetime supply.

"Oh, yes, she's always working hard. But lately she seems obsessed. Always in her head about something."

"You two are very close... for a bartender and the resort manager."

"You know Elizabeth. She's friendly with everyone."

"Sure," I said because, *No, Zai, Elizabeth was not friendly with everyone.* "When did Elizabeth start to get so stressed?"

"Maybe two weeks ago."

"What happened two weeks ago?"

Zai opened his mouth, but hesitated then pretended to hear something behind him. "I need to get back to work. Maybe you can give me your number and we can talk after I get off at 1 am?"

Only a twenty-two-ish man would think a 1 am meeting time was appropriate in any way. "I have your number — " I held up my marked arm — "I'll check in if I can. I would love to talk more about Elizabeth."

"Yes, *yes*... we really need to save her from making a terrible mistake." He kissed me on my cheek. Smelled like a commercial for piney body wash.

"Does that terrible mistake have to do with her husband?" I asked as he pulled away.

His face twisted into jealously. Always fascinating when the other man/woman believes they have the right to this emotion. Zai didn't like me seeing this side of him so he tried to twist back to his carefree adonis facade. But facade's are impossible to rebuild once we've seen what's underneath. "Ciao for now, Atheeeena."

Chapter Fifteen

ON MY WALK back through the hotel, I passed by the Nirvana Spa. A light was on in the back. Doubting anyone was getting naked at ten on a Saturday night — (I mean I doubt anyone was getting naked with a stranger... I *mean* I doubt anyone was getting a massage *here* at this hour) — I tried the door in hopes of getting a happy update from my doppelgänger.

"Diana?" I asked as I stepped inside. No answer. Only the chaotic clanging of someone navigating a small bathroom. "Diana..." I asked again, slipping past the desk and into the hall lit by orange bulbed wall pendants. The first room was the bathroom. Door closed. Emanating from the other side was either an overheating nuclear reactor or a woman in heels putting on make-up while crying.

"Diana?"

"I'm sorry!" she cried out because far too many women are taught it's their fault for being upset.

"It's Athena... from earlier... the writer..." *And your mother from another universe.*

This was met by stillness. Heels locked in place. Make-up application frozen. Even breathing put on hold. Then, in a burst, the door flung open, revealing a young woman in peak emotional crisis. A short black mini-skirt. (As in 'lower butt cheeks on display' short.) A tight red tank top bought because it failed completely at hiding the black bra which itself was bought for cleavage enhancement only. The heels were too tall for Diana or any woman with human DNA. Tears had fought recently applied mascara and won a bloody but decisive war for her face.

"I'm sorry it didn't go well."

"How'd you know?" she asked, sincerely, before self-awareness avalanched onto her head. Any tears that had managed to resist the urge to flee made a mad rush for the exit all it once. Her knees wobbled, I swooped in, caught her and lowered us with a few ounces of grace onto the closed (thankfully) toilet seat.

"You okay?" I asked.

"I just collapsed onto you!" Diana said.

"Only because I got nosy and barged into your post break-up revenge pre-party."

"You know he broke up with me, too? Is it the mini-skirt?"

"The waterfall of tears more than the outfit. But the two together left little doubt."

"Do you think he'll want to sleep with me after he sees me in this?"

"I mean, yes, duh, most men don't need a fraction as much inspiration. But it won't change his mind on staying with you. He's broken up with you because he's met someone else or because he thinks being with you is keeping him from meeting this someone else. You seducing him one last time may delay your own body's withdrawal symptoms for a few hours, but it will only speed up his desire to never see you again."

"How can you be only forty? You sounds so wise. Like you could be sixty."

· · ·

Forty. Forty?! FORTY?!??! I did some quick breath work to subdue the urge to throw my alternate-universe-daughter through the wall.

"I'm thirty-four," I mumbled, Diana mortified, I continued, "But maybe all the terrible men and their terrible break-ups, and my even-worse attempts to win them back has aged me inside and out."

"No, no, you look so good. Everyone older than twenty-five looks forty to me," Diana said and I latched onto that with zeal.

"How about this?" I said, standing us both up off the toilet. "I clean you up. Make that make-up work for you. Get you in an R-rated not X-rated revenge outfit and you promise me that you leave this hotel, go anywhere and with anyone as long as it's not back to the butthead that couldn't see how amazing you are."

She nodded. Sad. Then happy. Then more sad. Then sad and happy at the same time. We hugged and then I got to work.

· · ·

Probably couldn't start my own YouTube channel but I'll put my make-up skills up against most amateurs. As with too many things in my life, I do find I'm better at helping others with theirs than doing my own.

Diana let me convince her to exchange the skirt for jeans and I let her convince me the red tank and black bra now sold afterwork casual and not verge-of-psychotic break.

I insisted on walking her out to her car, largely because I wish someone had walked me away from my romantic tormenter during the too many times I had been in a too similar state.

I hugged her once beside her car. After she opened her door, she lunged back for another embrace. And while in this second hug, Diana whispered, "But if he's my soul mate, I can't really just move on, right?"

Pulled back, looked Diana into eyes that could be a mirror. *How many times had I thought that exact thought?* Only hearing her saying it finally allowed me to believe the bigger truth, "Did it break his heart to break your heart?"

"What do you mean?" Her confusion meant the answer was a no.

I explained, "I would like to believe most soul

mates, even if we have more than one, would never break our heart. But sometimes circumstances and timing make a relationship impossible. In these impossible relationships and their devastating break-ups, I would like to also believe that both the instigator and the receiver had equally broken hearts."

Diana stepped away from me, shaking her head as if shaking my words out of her brain. "You just don't understand him... he's not like other men..."

"I'm sure," I said because I was sure she was no longer in a place to hear that *all men are different yet all assholes are the same.*

"Maybe he didn't want to break up with me. Maybe he just wanted me to prove why we're meant to be with each other."

Oh boy. "Diana, like I said, sleeping with him one more time..."

"You're right. Not sex. He doesn't love sex that much anyway. Remember he's not like normal men! And I don't want a normal man anyway. I want him! And I just know I can prove to him our love is worth fighting for in more important ways."

. . .

I was doubting my ability to be a mother. At least to this daughter from another universe.

"Diana, let him go... and if you let him go, and he comes back, then *he* will have discovered you're worth fighting for. Far better and longer lasting than you convincing him."

"How many times has a guy you loved and then let go come back to you having discovered you're worth fighting for?"

Zero. Shit. She could read it on my face.

"I know I'm not old like you, Athena," she said, re-twisting that knife into my chest, "but I know I know this man better than you do and I know, deep down, he just needs to know that I'm the type of girl who will walk to the end of the universe for him."

My failure to instill any wisdom into Diana left me wondering if I had any wisdom inside me to instill. "Can you at least go home and sleep on it?"

She had to think about this. A long time. "You're right. I'll go home and sleep on it."

"Thank you."

"And tomorrow I will come back and win him back forever."

I smiled because any word that left my mouth would have been a lie or an act of war. Diana hugged me again, more drunk on her romantic delusions than before I intervened. Then she hopped in her car and sped off into the night.

If it was possible to make Diana's heartache more combustible, I had done it. Something my own mother had done countless times for me.

Chapter Sixteen

AS I RE-ENTERED the hotel lobby, Derek Shapiro, of Cornell University, re-entered my evening:

"How was your dinner, Ms. West?"

"Shouldn't you be helping with the bachelorette party on the 4th floor?" I pointed upwards.

"Female staff only."

"Ah. Understandable."

"Yes, very. Well, um, Ms. West, now that you've spoken with Ms. Diaz, can I assist by adding any additional knowledge?"

"Actually... " I had theories about Derek Shapiro of Cornell University that I'd like to test. But by the time the words got to my mouth, I decided fate had brought me to San Evita, California to heal old wounds not disembowel self-righteous assistant managers. "I think I'll be able to figure most of it out myself."

"That," Derek started and just couldn't help himself from finishing with, "I seriously doubt. But good luck." Derek Shapiro of Cornel University spun on his heels and retreated behind the check-in desk. He yelled at the young lady working it because someone with boobs needed to suffer for his insecurities.

Plopped myself deep into a lobby couch that could finance a college education and tried to get inside the head of a man I had spent the past sixteen years trying to get out of my head.

Where would a thirty-five year old Travis Diaz be on a Friday night? Elizabeth insinuated he would be findable. I had to believe that meant somewhere on resort grounds.

If he was half the dramatic poet he longed to be, he'd be sitting on the beach with a notebook in his hands, tears of existential anguish dropping from eyes to page.

If he had the talent to write a book alone, he'd be

in his room typing a world into life and the night into dawn.

If he was the legendary lover he briefly convinced Hollywood he was, Travis would be finding a willing victim in the Ocean Cafe Bar...

If he...

Wait.

Of course.

So where would I find thirty-five year old Travis Diaz? The same place I'd find seventeen year-old Travis.

Finding me first.

"Hello, Athena." A voice that once upon a time could change my body chemistry with two words.

My body informed me that time was upon me yet again.

Years Ago

Eighteen Years In Fact
(a millennia ago to be more exact)

Chapter Seventeen

*THE FIRST TRAVIS HIGH SCHOOL
CHAPTER

IMAGINE you went to high school with one of the Beatles. Not a Beatle before they were famous. Post-Ed Sullivan show Beatles (apologies to anyone not steeped into pop cultural history) yet still in high school.

Now imagine this Beatle was ALSO Tom Brady. (He's the only past or present NFL quarterback I can name so he'll have to do.) And not forty-something Tom Brady but a teenage Tom Brady but still famous like he already dumped Giselle and was sleeping with some Kardashian between starring in a million commercials.

Yeah, so a Paul McCartney-Tom Brady computer generated super nova of talent, charm, and hotness so potent it should come with a warning label.

Yeah, so imagine all that, and *then* let me tell you that Elizabeth Holden had let her eyes linger on Travis at least seven times (and those are just the ones I witnessed) and he never noticed or, worse, he noticed and didn't care.

Travis' band — *Honey Nuts* — had not one, not two, but three songs in the Variety show even though no single act was supposed to have more than one. In defense of Mrs. Bradbury, *Honey Nuts* was already Chicago famous and I'm sure she had secret illegal fantasies about Travis just like every other woman with a heartbeat. (He could pass for twenty-five despite being seventeen.)

This meant that for the six dress rehearsals and four days of live performances, I'd be back stage with Travis. Back stage in my tight black attire. And, sure, there were fifty other kids back there, too, but he had started to let *his eyes* linger on *me* amidst the chaos... and those eyes with that perfect face with that perfect body with that perfect voice. Yeah, it gave me a heart attack. It thumped so fast and so hard I just assumed I'd die. Once home that first night I tried to untie the shy Athena so she could pretend Travis's gaze was meaningless but even shy Athena insisted, '*He's too beautiful. Maybe him staring at you will kill us but it'll be worth it*' and she tied herself back up.

So the next night I stared back. And each night after that I'd do the same thing, each time growing more confident in my gaze. Those ten days of silent stares across the crowded dressing room evolved from awkward to flirtatious to epic eye-sex.

After the last performance, I assumed Travis would never look at me again. Assumed that I was one of a million girls Travis made passionate eye-love with and then never gazed upon again.

But on Sunday morning at 8:03 AM, Travis parked his goddamn motorcycle on my goddamn lawn, knocked on my goddamn door, and said, "Want to go for a ride?" You can't even get a motor-cycle license in Illinois until you're eighteen! But I nodded a minuscule, exploding yes and we spent hours weaving through suburban streets, my arms gripped around his waist, my pelvis against his tail-bone. (I didn't orgasm. But if I knew what I knew now, I could have.)

If he had taken me to his house or even a van he rented for the hour and tore off my clothes I would have succumbed with enthusiastic cluelessness. But, no. Travis didn't want my body. If only he did.

Travis drove us to Lake Michigan. Took me by

the hand with a small blanket hidden under his motorcycle seat. Found an isolated sandy hill, laid the blanket down, took my hands in his, unfurled those eyes of his upon my own from eleven inches away and said, "When I first heard you perform your poem, I felt something so deep, so incredible, I didn't know how to explain what I was feeling. It's taken me weeks to work up the courage to ask to talk to you about it. It's just that I'm a writer too —" *Yeah, duh, you have seven songs on the radio, Travis!* "— and I'd love to get inside the heart and mind of a writer as brilliant as you."

I mean, come on.

COME ON.

Would any girl — or even the straightest of boys! — not have fallen in love with the football stud / music star / super model telling you all he wants to do his hold your hand at the beach and talk about how brilliant you are?

I was so screwed.

Yes, I fell in love with him instantly. Didn't know enough about love to realize I had. But I did. And nothing I have felt for any man or woman or cat or cookie since has come even close.

He'd call me every day after school. Or just show up on his motorcycle. And when there's a boy like

Travis taking up all your free time you forget that your abandoned best friend Elizabeth might be slowly plotting to destroy your life in your absence.

I was the one who kissed Travis. (Three weeks after the beach — I would have self-combusted waiting for him to make the first move.) I was the one who put his hands on my boobs and the one who asked to unbutton his pants and the one to buy condoms and the one to google how to do it right.

So yes, it turns out I was the nerdy girl who was secretly the super horny girl. And Travis was the Greek god who was more comfortable writing songs with me than making out with me. But I thought this was normal. (I mean, maybe it would be great if it was!) And Travis and I flew through the end of my sophomore year and most of junior year as only soul mates can fly.

We planned out our wedding, named our children, and promised each other we would kill ourselves if anything tragic ever happened to the other. Because, as teenage Travis explained, '*When soul mates can't live in this life together they must find each other in the next life.*'

My once romance famished heart had now become addicted to love and each declaration needed higher stakes, bigger gestures, grander designs to make me feel as deeply as my heart demanded.

I would have done anything for our love. I would have done anything for Travis.

Anything...

But then...

Oh, yes, *but then*...

Friday Night

at the
Desmond
Diamond
Hotel

10:32 PM

Chapter Eighteen

I STOOD up from the hotel's lobby couch, stepped a tiny step back as Travis stepped a big step forward. As if he was a predator and I the prey debating the pros and cons of being eaten.

He said, "Can I have a hug so I can re-connect to the person I was and the person I still hope to be?"

His words were a mirage. I know that now.

I *should* know that now.

And I'm gonna say '*No, Travis, you can't have a hug after you broke my heart, married my best friend, and stole millions of dollars from me*'.

I'm gonna say no.

I should say no.

I can say no, right?

I can!

"Okay," I said because my boundaries never learned how to do their job. Might have been easier to reject him if time had worn on thirtysomething Travis Diaz like it had Elizabeth. If social media filters had been doing all the work they do for everyone else. But nope. He was as gorgeous at thirty-five as he was at seventeen. Maybe more so. For the rareness of true natural beauty was lost on teenage Athena.

His embrace was a time machine.

I was a girl again. I was in the arms of a boy who loved me. Who understood me. Who will always be there for me. I tried to sink deeper into the hug. Maybe if I sunk deep enough I won't have to grow up. I'll pull back and be eighteen again. Be able to re-live my life with the wisdom painfully gained.

Then he pulled away, snapping me back to my very present day cosmic sadness. Travis opened his mouth, paused, thought, then said, "Can we take a walk outside and down to the beach? My thoughts and feelings are much clearer when closer to nature."

This was a trap. The hug had given him an easy way to spring it. Travis loved locations where he was comfortable and you weren't. Gave him a sense of confidence and control. But I was too curious to know why he wanted to talk to me outside the hotel to say no. "Sure, Travis. You can take me to the beach... again."

"Again? Oh, that's right... we went to Lake Michigan on our first date. I didn't know it was a date. I thought it was two young artists getting to know each other."

"Oh, Travis... do you want me to pretend I'm as naive as I was back then? I can if it helps you say whatever you need to say."

A blankness covered his face. Like a computer freezing from a foreign command.

"Just take me to the beach, Travis. I won't complicate your plan any more."

He smiled, thankful but not fully understanding why he was thankful.

(Or pretending not to understand. Travis was smart enough to know the advantages of pretending to be an attractive simpleton.)

Then, without another word, my first boyfriend led us past a leering Derek at the front desk, out of the hotel, into the night, down the hill, across a bridge, over the Pacific Coast Highway, and to the ocean's edge.

When he finally turned and faced me, I half expected he would kiss me. Half of me wanted him to. Maybe more than half.

But the look in his eyes was not, alas, carnal longing.

I wouldn't have kissed him anyway!
Probably.
Liar.
I totally would have.
Ugh.
Gross.
Pathetic.
So pathetic.
Maybe I should kiss him.
Stop it!
In my defense, another theory of mine is that the

first person that shares your first great orgasm haunts every subsequent sexual encounter. We are then doomed to spend our lives in desperate search for their equal. They become our own very personal Moby Dick. (Or/and Moby Vagina depending on your tastes.)

Travis was my very, very *moby* dick.

But with the sand beneath us, the ocean crashing with transcendence beside us, there was no lust in his face. No sexual tension in his body.

There *was* love in his eyes. But the broken love of a broken heart.

Broken heart?

But he was the one who broke mine!

Thirty-four year old me wanted to be wise enough to dismiss this as an act meant to manipulate me to his ends. Yet I knew for Travis his emotions *were* real. He felt big, dreamt big, loved big. For his appeal to me in high school and — I must now confess — to me still was more than his excruciating gorgeousness. After years and years of trying to squeeze drops of feeling from souls hiding in the smallness of life, the larger than the universe force that was Travis was an ocean for my creative, romantic, and sensual needs to dive into.

His words: "Athena, we made a baby together. A beautiful, beautiful baby. And then you abandoned that baby. And I had to raise our child alone, without your help. I did my best. But a baby needs a mother and a father..." Tears formed in his eyes. "Our baby needed you... and our baby needs you still."

I said out loud what I now knew was the real reason I was in San Evita:

"You want me to write the sequel with you, don't you?"

Years Ago

Sixteen If You Count By Years
(Yesterday if You Count By
Rawness of the Emotions)

Chapter Nineteen

THE SPRING of his senior year, Travis tore his ACL playing Quidditch with me. He decided this was a sign to de-commit from the Ohio State football scholarship, stay in Riverbend while I finished high school, work on his music, and then go to college wherever I went. (Even at the time I knew, despite the grand romance of it, this was an idiotic life decision.)

And maybe this irresponsible plan would have worked out if not for all the *Honey Nuts* songs being pulled from the local radio stations once the established artists' he stole all the melodies from got word of this suburban kid's maybe innocent/maybe not-so-innocent theft.

They even pulled the song version he produced

of my *Dreams Die After Dinner*. It got lumped in with his crude rip-offs, a sad fate for my great poem I still ache over.

My timeless first love to the gorgeous athletic artist was now a co-dependent relationship with a nineteen year-old college drop out who smoked pot all day while I was in high school and then begged me all night to write a novel with him.

Which I did!

Sorta because he wouldn't make-out with me until after we wrote at least five hundred words. But mostly because Travis always got what he wanted.

nd Travis never wanted my heart.

Or my body.

He wanted my ideas. My talent. My proficient typing skills.

he book was terrible. Of course it was. He was stoned, I was horny, and neither of us had any idea what we were doing. But we provided just enough raw emotional truth (and I threw in all the fun high school melodrama and functional prose) that Travis convinced himself it was a masterpiece. And since I was the one who had actually read every book assigned to us in high school plus a thousand more, I was the one who had to tell him, *No, Travis, the book is crap.* Teenage crap. When he asked if he could send it to publishers, I said absolutely not. I was already working on my first *literary* novel that would, surely, win the Pulitzer and all the other awards I hadn't heard of. But it would only win if no one knew I'd never written something as grotesquely bad as *Confessions of a Teenage Broken Heart.*

So of course the literary gods for their own cruel, comical reasons made *Confessions* a famous best seller and even more famous Netflix series. After that I wished everyone knew I'd written it. How do *you* not know I was the co-writer of the novel? In fact, that I'd typed 94% of the actual words? Well, that's where Elizabeth comes in.

Travis's insistence that *Confessions* was a great book, combined with the rest of his downfall, probably/kinda/sorta had the tiniest part of me thinking that he was not, in fact, my soul mate who I would spend eternity with.

But I had promised eternity to him!

And when you promise someone eternity, even at seventeen, you must keep that promise! (Cold-hearted, cool-headed note to my younger readers: you absolutely do *not* need to keep that promise.)

Well without football and his band, all Travis had was our dumb book. And I kept insisting it was the *dumbest* book. (I mean, admit some of the dialogue in the show, if you removed the music, would embarrass you to say alone in bed with the lights off.)

And, I would learn, when a boy can't find self-esteem in sports or school or work, that boy — whether he's nineteen or twenty-nine or thirty-nine — is going to find self-esteem in another woman.

It's just that this other woman, in this case, was my best friend Elizabeth.

Yes, I had gone from an overly devoted BFF to AWOL for that first year after the Travis Era began. But what girl or boy experiencing first love hasn't gone through a phase of abandoning their friends? I started working my way back to Elizabeth by the end of junior year. And she provided an oasis from broken Travis for me our senior year. I thought we were stronger than ever!

But in April, two months before graduation, on the first warm spring day, Elizabeth and I decided to drive a couple towns over to the Glenview Dairy Bar and have chocolate dipped soft serve. Only stoned Travis had stalked us there. When we first noticed him hiding across the street in a park gazebo, I told Elizabeth, "I don't mean this but sometimes I wish Travis would dump me so I wouldn't have to dump him."

The shock on her face probably should have sent flares to my head. "But he's *so* hot, Athena."

"Yeah... sorta... but also maybe being hot isn't always the coolest thing..."

Travis could tell we were talking about him, crossed the street toward us, and before Elizabeth could drag me away to her car,

I yelled, "Travis, you can't stalk people."

"But I love you," he said to me.

Yet I was looking at Elizabeth as the words left him. Her face flushed to the faintest of pinks. I spun toward Travis. He couldn't look at her. I could sense his organs contorting even as his body remained focused on me.

My eyes bounced between them in rapid, information gulping seconds.

And I knew.

Knew they were sleeping together.

I puked on the spot, burst into tears, and ran seven miles back to my mother's house.

The first man I loved and might have stayed with forever despite all else and the first woman I loved and might have married if my bi-sexuality were truly embraced had, behind my back, met, gotten naked, and made love. Or fucked. Or just had really, really bad sex. Still no idea which. Never spoke to either of them again... until yesterday.

Nineteen months later after puking outside Dairy Bar, I discovered in a Mrs. Bradbury Facebook post that Travis and Elizabeth had gotten married in San Diego. This re-opened wounds and then made a few new ones. I thought they had an affair because both wanted *more of me*! But now it was because *they* were the soul mates and I was just the pit stop before the final destination.

Two years after their wedding, a lawyer offered me ten thousand dollars to give up all rights to *Confessions of a Teenage Broken Heart*. I had already completed the novel that would make me millions (I was sure) so I laughed, signed the contract, and took the money.

Only Elizabeth was smart enough to see the zeitgeist potential of the book. She put herself as co-writer, found them an agent, and sold it to a publisher. That it turned first into a best seller and then into one of Netflix's first mega-hits no one — not even Elizabeth — could have predicted.

The ten grand they paid me? Greatest heist in literary history. Book sold millions of copies, Netflix bought it for fortune, and they got a book deal for a sequel worth seven figures.

The interviews they did for the book quickly exposed Elizabeth as the non-writer which made it easy for Hollywood to crown Travis and his over-the-top romantic notion of art as the next great literary genius. He 'amicably separated' from Elizabeth and entered into a short, burning cycle of dating actresses and musicians (even rumors about Taylor Swift but no way Taylor would fall for his faux artist's heart).

Then his star fell with the show. He never wrote a second book. But for some reason, Elizabeth was there to catch him. They bought the resort, and, thanks to social media, gave me years more of insecurity and resentment to work through.

Friday Night

at the
Desmond
Diamond
Hotel

10:55 PM

Chapter Twenty

"You cheated on me with my best friend, Travis. I can't just drop my life in Chicago and write a book with you."

(I mean, I couldn't, right?)

"The greatest mistake of my life..."
"You married my best friend and she helped you become a famous millionaire writer. I think it worked out for ya, Trav."

"I married her because she promised to help raise our baby after you abandoned it."

"It's just a book."

"Just a book? Just a book!? It has touched the hearts and lives of millions of teenagers. Helped them understand all that they hope and fear and dream and desire. And it has done all of this without its mom."

"Because you did it without me."

"I took our baby away from you in a moment of fear that you would smother it with a pillow. Murder it before the world could meet it."

"Your metaphor is a bit much."

"You always hated my metaphors."

"I didn't hate them." Yes, I did. They were cheap ketchup on an expensive steak. (Pot. Kettle.)

"Athena, you know why Elizabeth really brought you here, don't you?"

"No." Well, yes, maybe I did now. But I wanted to hear his side.

"Because she knows my book is more important than anything. More than the hotel. More than even my marriage. So she brought you here afraid I was going to leave her for someone else who could help finish the sequel…"

"*Have* you been writing with someone else?"

"How could I write it with anyone but you?" He said avoiding an answer with a question. "A child needs its real mom."

"Travis..."

"Our baby — *Confessions of a Teenage Broken Heart* — it's time for it to grow up... and it will only grow up if you agree to write the sequel with me."

Closed my eyes. Fast forwarded through all the possible timelines of my life from this moment forward. Saying yes would be a disaster. I only wrote the first novel with him because I was sleeping with him so to write the sequel I'd definitely have to sleep with him again. Except now he's married to my ex-best friend and I'm a year shy of geriatric pregnancies. Sure, Elizabeth would deserve the payback. But she might not even see it as payback! She might be happy to share her husband with me if that meant I was writing the book neither of them could write and helping them cash those sequel checks they (and probably the hotel) desperately needed.

I'm sure I'd get paid pennies to their dollars. I'm sure my name would be in tiny print compared to theirs. I'm sure I wouldn't even be invited to meetings with those glitzy Hollywood types.

I'd hate myself for saying yes. Hate Travis if he fell back in love with me. Hate him more if he didn't. Hate Elizabeth for being willing to share me with Travis. Trapping me into this bizarre, desperate love triangle.

So of course I had to say no. Go back to Chicago. Rebuild my life by finally letting go of Elizabeth Holden and Travis Diaz forever.

"Okay. I'll do it. I'll write the sequel with you."

And then Travis kissed me. Knew he would. He couldn't help it. If our lives were a book that promised happy endings, almost every writer would have insisted our characters kiss.

The truth was that I said yes not just because writing the sequel would save me, however briefly, from my loveless, jobless life in Chicago. The truth was I said yes because at that exact moment I wanted to be kissed by a beautiful man beside a moonlit ocean. I wanted that more than I wanted to be smart or safe or sane.

Saturday Morning

COFFEE
WITH
DETECTIVE BLUE

7:17 AM

Chapter Twenty-One

TOOK A SIP OF MY LATTE. It was below average. No wonder the Desmond Diamond Hotel was failing.

"Ms. West, I assume Travis Diaz will confirm this conversation on the beach happened as you say?" Blue was finally taking notes. Maybe he had needed a coffee, too.

"Yes. Travis deceives but he rarely lies."

"How did he deceive you?"

"Are you married, Detective Blue?"

"Not relevant."

"Maybe if you're married it would help you understand the mind of a married man."

"I'm not... married," Blue said. Gonna forget that loaded pause. Plus he had no ring. Or even an indent of a ring. Only self delusion can get us through sometimes. "So how did Travis deceive you?"

"Travis elevates every moment with you to such heights that it makes you feel like you're living a movie version of your own life. The romance. The drama. The emotional stakes. All dialed to eleven. Every moment is special. Every breath shared with him feels vital to the meaning of the universe."

"And that's deceptive how?"

"Because Travis really only thinks his life is special. The rest of us are just supporting characters, useful only to his protagonist's arc. But we don't realize we're supporting characters until he's done with us. Until we've done things for that feeling he and he alone makes us feel. And here's the thing about being a supporting character in someone's else's story: sometimes we are useful alive... and sometimes we're more useful dead."

Friday Night

at the
Desmond
Diamond
Hotel

11:19 PM

Chapter Twenty-Two

Sugar is my drug of choice. So I can't call Travis's kiss heroin. For me the kiss was like a piece of Bakers Square French Silk pie twenty years after all the locations within fifty miles had closed.

Then Travis pulled away. Our lips parted. Erupting volcano-level shame for kissing the married man who had broken my trust of all men. But the shame was a distant second place to the ache that ached: *No, no, no, I need more pie than that.*

"I love you, Athena West."

Before I could decide if he meant that or was just reading dialogue the universe had written for him, his phone rang. He looked at the caller ID. Sent it to voicemail.

"Who was that?"

"A distraction from our destiny." *Travis doesn't lie, he deceives*. He took my hand in his. "You must be getting cold. Let's get back to the hotel and begin planning out the rest of our lives."

I wasn't cold. But whoever had called his phone needed him inside the hotel. I let him lead me back away from the ocean, back across the Pacific Coast Highway, and into the hotel he owned with his wife.

Half way through our walk, he began to unload all his thoughts for the sequel to *Confessions of a Teenage Broken Heart*. It was more download than unload. He had so, *so* many ideas. As if it was the only thing he had thought about since we last wrote sixteen years ago. He had never stopped obsessing over our fictional characters and their fictional drama. Just as I had never stopped obsessing over him and Elizabeth and their very real betrayal.

Once back in the lobby, he took out his phone again. After a couple clicks, Travis said, "I just sent you all my notes for the sequel. It's over a hundred pages. No one can understand what I've written down but I know you will and that's why I knew it could only be you."

"Okay," I said because the profound regret of every decision I had made the past twenty four hours was short-circuiting my ability to think or say anything else.

He whispered, "I can't kiss you again in the hotel. You understand. Of course you understand, babe. But you go up to your room and start working on the book and I'll come visit you after I take care of some... hotel business."

Didn't say anything. Couldn't even nod my head.

"Smile. You're so much prettier when you smile. I hate when you're serious. I know you're happy, Athena. I can tell. I know you better than anyone. I know you're a woman who can only be happy with a man like me." He blew an invisible kiss that would have hit the ground three feet short of my feet, turned and zoomed off toward the Ocean Cafe.

Considered doing as Travis said. Retreat into my hotel room, into his notes, into his larger-than-life life as if we were still teenagers.

Considered it for about eight seconds.

Because as soon as my ex disappeared from

view, the spell he cast — cast by his body, by his kiss, and by our history — vanished with him.

And because every relationship since Travis had taught me that as soon as someone begs you to make them your whole world you should immediately blow that world the fuck up.

Saturday Morning

COFFEE
WITH
DETECTIVE BLUE

7:29 AM

Chapter Twenty-Three

"AND TRAVIS LEFT you in the lobby at what time?" Blue asked, studying my eyes. I liked him studying me. Even if he was looking for evidence that I was a killer. It allowed me to study his eyes. Look for evidence that he could fall in love with me. Despite the circumstances. Or even because of them.

"Eleven thirty," I said as I thought other things.

"Elizabeth was dead less than two hours later."

"Yes, she was."

"Ms. West, sixteen years after your high school boyfriend cheated on you with your high school best friend, you show up at a hotel they bought with money you insist they stole. Stole from a book you insist you wrote. Then ninety minutes after you kiss this now married man, his wife — your ex-best friend — ends up murdered."

"Yep. It's quite an unbelievable story."

It really was. Like maybe *too* unbelievable? If I were to write this into a novel, I'd have to change some things. Definitely couldn't have my character fall in love with the Detective trying to convict me of murder.

(Or I'd have to admit I'm a love addict. First I'd have to admit it to myself, then get it diagnosed by someone besides my mother, and have this addiction ruin my life more than it already has. Character development is a bitch.)

"Ms. West, what are you writing down? Looked into him. Those eyes. They held me like strong arms might if I had weak knees. I didn't say that. Even two people meant for each other can't tell each other everything. Instead I said, "I can turn this into a novel, right?"

"What do you mean?"

"I mean, it's my life and I don't need to get

permission to use any of this material for a book, right?"

"Your friend is dead, likely by your hand. You will spend the rest of your life in prison... and all you're thinking about is writing a book about all of it?" (*No, Detective Blue, that's not all I'm thinking about. I've been thinking about kissing you and that mustache of yours since you sat down across from me.*)

Yet again, I said slightly less crazy things, "Well, being locked in a cell might be the only way I could stop myself from procrastinating." Winked at him.

"Ms. West." Blue's last patience with me slipped out the door.

"Mr. Blue."

"We're both tired. I think it's time we draw our conversation to an end."

"You're right. It's time for me to tell you what really happened."

"Thank you."

"But can you first admit if you weren't a detective and I wasn't your prime suspect — "

"Only suspect."

"—*only* suspect. Right. Well, if not for those two things, would you acknowledge the chemistry between us?"

"Ms. West."

"Fine. I get it. Hard to say that out loud. But. Wink. Wink. Our eyes can say it."

And our eyes did. Detective Blue would deny it even to his own reflection. But I've gone on enough dates (*we might be approaching a thousand, people*) and had gotten naked with enough men (*fifty-something I believe. Don't judge unless you're judging me sexually empowered then judge away*) that my eyes, brain, and heart knew when two bodies liked each other. And my body and Detective Blue's... they liked each other.

But he had to say, "Ms. West, I don't believe you're well. I think you know this. And I think that's why you want to tell me what happened last night."

"Okay. I will. I'll tell you."

"Thank you."

"But I want you to know that I'll still want to kiss you even though I had to solve this murder for you."

PART THREE

THE FINAL DEATH

Friday Night

at the
Desmond
Diamond
Hotel

11:41 PM

Chapter Twenty-Four

As Travis disappeared from view, I opened the *Confessions* sequel document he had emailed. One hundred and eight pages. Yet I knew within a paragraph that Travis hadn't written much of this. If any.

I have one strong belief when it comes to writing styles. Great writers — and not just the famous ones, but also every original voice out there that has never been discovered and may never be — all posses styles unique to them and them alone. Like fingerprints. Impossible to mistake for another. And yet all bad writers — and this includes many, *many* famous ones — are almost indistinguishable from one another. There's nothing alive in their words. It's just plot pooping more plot. It's sudoku for people who like their puzzles with letters instead of numbers.

And this document Travis had sent me couldn't be his because the language breathed, moved, danced, fucked, and screamed. They were words assembled by a great writer and Travis was great only at pretending to be a great writer. Before I could tell my own head who the real writer had to be —

— the annoyingly familiar voice of no one's favorite Ivy League graduate clogged up my mind with: "Mr. Diaz asked that I escort you back to your room so that you can get started on your work."

Twisted on my heel to face him. Gosh, he got less attractive by the hour. By morning he might be a squashed toad. "Derek…"

"Yes, Ms. West?"

"Your parents are Hugh and Debbie Shapiro of the HGTV show *Hotel Hospital* that got cancelled in 2012 — "

"No…" His eyes searched for an escape hatch.

"That wasn't a question. I only had a short time to look you up after our elevator visit, but I'm assuming your parents' divorce was difficult. On you personally, but also their small but eclectic portfolio of Arizona hospitality properties. Your dad find new investors? Looking to make a comeback through a hotel his son has been staking out?"

"You think you've got it all figured out, don't you? Childless, unmarried women north of thirty usually do because they have so much time on their hands." Derek took an aggressive step toward me. Men always try to act big when they feel small.

I said, "Thank you for that. Answered my last question."

"And what question was that?" Derek's face promised if murdering women who pissed off sexists was legal, I'd be dead.

"How you planned to steal the hotel from Elizabeth."

Derek Shapiro of Cornel University turned a deep shade of purple as his teeth were at last sheathed. For a moment he begged all the gods he had briefly worshipped for the words to defeat me but they all ignored his pleas.

To his silence, I added, "Don't worry, Derek. Before I leave here I'm sure I'll have an opportunity to tell you how I figured you out so easily."

His purple face managed to squeeze out, "Ms. West, please return to your room as ordered." He grabbed me by the elbow. Pinched it until I flinched.

PTSD of ex-boyfriends who communicated in violence when my words outgunned them.

As his grip clenched down on my arm, I managed to say, "Here's the best part about a man like you, Derek Shapiro of Cornell University — you remind a woman like me why it's been so easy to stay single." This insult required a moment to process. A rarity for him. I used his shock of experiencing contemplation to yank free from his clasp and then out of his sight.

Chapter Twenty-Five

With Derek left behind in the lobby, I went down the hotel's north hall. The same direction Travis had gone.

Instead of shops offering merchandise I couldn't afford, the hall was lined with windows offering pool and mountain views I couldn't afford. Because I knew one thing for sure: Elizabeth and Travis weren't inviting me back once I told them I wasn't writing the sequel for them.

The cafe's entrance was as large as Angelico's was small. A giant circular bar in the center, surrounded by tables, then walls of endless giant glass sliders opening to the pool and a patio with a daytime view of the ocean. But at this hour, it was just a view of darkness so intense you had to remind yourself this wasn't the end of the galaxy.

Three people at the bar. One bartender. Every table empty. It was late. Almost midnight. Maybe that alone excused the lack of patrons. Maybe.

With no sight of Travis, I gave myself permission to enter the kitchen. One cook and one waitress sharing a joint. Their brains panicked at sight of me but before they could decide if I was in the wrong place or they were in the wrong, I said, "Travis said I could find him back here — "

Relieved, the waitress pointed out the door to the back. I gave a thumbs up 'cuz thumbs up are impossible to dislike.

The exit out of the cafe kitchen left me on a thin stone path that forked at once. One direction led back along the side of the hotel. The smarter choice. The other up into the shadowy, wooded mountainside. The suicidal choice.

With the end-of-the-galaxy blackness now enveloping all my senses including the common one, I ventured up the path and into a forest that was probably a favorite camping spot for werewolves.

. . .

But twenty yards into the forest, the trees thinned, revealing a tiny village of tinier mountainside cabins. Counted eleven of them. My dimly lit stone path split off every few steps toward the front door of each.

Ten of the cabins were dark. Half suffering in the final death throes of broken windows, caved roofs, missing doors. All cried out for love and attention and modern plumbing.

One cabin's front room was lit. Whatever and whoever was inside hidden behind a closed curtain. Against my natural survival and human decency instincts, I tiptoed off the path and around the far side of the lit window. My heart raced because I'm meant to be hiding behind a computer screen not sneaking around California hotel grounds at midnight.

I do not know what I feared more — finding Travis inside the cabin or finding a stranger and then that stranger finding me. Didn't matter. My legs demanded I find out one way or another.

Pressed my back against the cabin, then braved a turn of my head and a lean of my eyes until I could see inside...

Elizabeth. Shirt off. Bra on. Buttoning her suit pants. Was that a six pack? Most women with perfect abs post pictures of them weekly. Not Elizabeth. She had more important things to do than upload thirst traps for strangers. Or ex-best friends stalking them two thousand miles away.

I should turn away.

Right?

This wasn't what I was looking for. I was looking for Travis. Looking for Travis and whoever seduced him away from our ocean edge kiss back to the hotel. Maybe it was Elizabeth? She was talking to someone. Couldn't hear what she was saying. But someone was inside the cabin with her.

It had to be Travis.

Of course.

They needed me to write their sequel so they could cash their sequel checks and save their ailing hotel. All this drama to get me out to their hotel was simply a ruse to once again ensnare my talents and heart for their grander ambitions.

But then Lilith stormed out from the bathroom.

Lilith?

In underwear and nothing else.

Lilith!

She yelled. That I could hear.

A lot of 'You promised me, Liz!'

Liz?

I never called her Liz. No one ever called her Liz. Maybe if I hadn't listened to my mother all those years ago I'd be the one who got to see that stomach up close and call her Liz.

Lilith was angry and emotional and yet looked camera ready for an erotic thriller, proving one of my theories that most women in their early twenties have no idea how time, gravity, and calories actually work.

Lilith lunged at Elizabeth. I didn't look away. I should have looked away. But my eyes would have never listened to me anyway.

She kissed her. Kissed my best friend. My ex-best friend. The wife of my ex-boyfriend. Elizabeth didn't fight it for a moment. And in that one moment, I ached for the passion and lust and pain that fueled them both.

But then Elizabeth pulled away. And looked *right at me*.

Uhhhhhhhhhh —-

Stumbled backwards as if her eyes shot a bullet through my chest. Fell over a fallen branch, hit the ground hard. Might have yelped. Definitely yelped. What does a yelp even sound like? More like a 'yiiiieeep!' But no one would know what a yiiiieeep was so I'll call it a yelp.

And the yelp led quickly to:

Elizabeth opening the cabin door, unbuttoned blouse covering what it could. She said, "Athena?"

And I said, "No?" and prayed.

Saturday Morning

COFFEE
WITH
DETECTIVE BLUE

7:38 AM

Chapter Twenty-Six

AN ANNOYED BLUE BLURTED OUT, "But *you* said the last time you saw Elizabeth alive was when she left Angelico's."

"Oh. Right. Am I an unreliable narrator?" This formed in my brain as a genuine question but by the time it left my mouth there was no way Blue could interpret it as such.

"Stop fucking around, Ms. West! This is not a joke!"

"Sorry. You're right. It's just that I didn't know if I was going to tell you about seeing her again." Again, this felt less obnoxious in my head than outside of it.

"You can't just decide what you can tell me or not tell me!"

"You're frustrated." (And remember I like frustrating men.)

"I'm livid. What else have you been hiding from me?"

"I haven't told you about my mother's weakness for Moscow Mules or the time I cheated on my ethics final or my first threesome..."

"Ms. West. What else haven't you told me about your activities since you arrived at the hotel?"

"I didn't tell you about the eight times I went pee, or the two times I pooped, or about what I always do in hotel showers when alone and single — "

"Ms. West!" He cut me off before I told him more than he was ready to hear. "*What else* are you hiding that is relevant to the murder of *your* best friend?"

"Well, I didn't think Elizabeth having an affair with Lilith was relevant because you said she alibi'd out."

"But you said I didn't like her alibi!"

"Yes, of course I did because I can read your every thought but it's not my job to convince you what information is useful to your case."

Blue dropped his chin to his chest, unable to look at me. I might have pushed too far.

So I offered, "I'm sorry. I'm enjoying our time

together and might be a bit flippant considering the situation."

"How can you be so flippant with your life at stake?"

"Are you going to kill me?"

"In some states, murderers still get the death penalty."

"Yes, but you and I both know that the death penalty only helps psychopaths rationalize violence and whoever is found guilty of murdering Elizabeth will never face such an archaic sentence."

"Ms. West…" He needed a nap. Most men did after this much Athena West before eight am. Or eight pm for that matter.

"Detective Blue…"

"What time did Elizabeth catch you spying on her at the cabin?"

"Must have been 12:15 or so."

"So Lilith left…"

"Yes. Good guess."

"And after she left, you went inside the cabin with Elizabeth."

"Oooh. You should be a detective."

"And then something she said or something you discussed led to a disagreement and, in a fit of anger, you stabbed her in the back when she tried to leave the cabin.”

“The photograph you showed me suggested Elizabeth was stabbed from behind while she was heading back into the cabin.”

Blue scrunched his lips so high they almost touched his nose.

To his exasperation, I offered temporary relief in the form of, “So maybe I had taken a knife from the Ocean Cafe kitchen when I passed through, hidden it in the back of my pants, and then, after this supposed conversation with Elizabeth, she kicked me out of the cabin only when she turned around, I leapt at her, knife first, and plunged it into her back.”

The profound pride that over took Blue’s face was the same most men had after I orgasmed. *Sorry, dude, but ease back on your self-satisfaction. I did all the work while you just laid underneath me and looked pretty.*

“Or, Detective Blue, it went absolutely nothing like that...”

Friday Night

at the
Mountainside Cabins
at the
Desmond
Diamond
Hotel

12:08 AM

(So, technically, Early Saturday Morning)

Chapter Twenty-Seven

"Her?" A now half dressed Lilith said as she stepped outside the cabin and beside Elizabeth. "Are you breaking up with me because of *her*?" The disgust in Lilith's voice screamed *she's so old and fat and unsophisticated compared to me!*

Elizabeth didn't answer Lilith. Just stood still. Chin down. Eyes open. Her assistant and lover and maybe now ex-lover got the hint. Lilith retreated into the cabin, grabbed shoes and her suit jacket, then raced past Elizabeth, down the stone path, and back toward the hotel. Young, smart, ambitious women can fight tears better than most. But even Lilith would lose this battle. Elizabeth had that kind of power.

Once alone, Elizabeth looked up toward the

night sky and asked, "Can we talk?" and then disappeared into the cabin. I followed. Of course I did.

The cabin was warm yellows and burnt oranges, hard timber and tidy corners. Smaller than my small living room and yet I couldn't stop from thinking that I could build my entire life from inside here. Elizabeth would run her hotel, I'd write with Ripper on my lap, take walks to the ocean with our shelter rescued puppy, and then we'd make love and watch Christmas movies every night of the year.

"What are you thinking about?" Elizabeth asked as she finished buttoning up her blouse.

For perhaps the first time in my life, I didn't speak when someone I loved asked me that question.

To my silence, she said, "You found Travis…"

"I did."

"Did you find out who he's sleeping with?" Elizabeth was a child caught with cookies in her mouth hoping against hope that no one noticed who emptied the jar.

"Elizabeth. Come on. Lilith and Zai — "

"How'd you know about Zai?"

I offered my quickest *'you know that's my super-power, woman'* flare of my eyes then continued with, "You don't care who he's sleeping with. I'm guessing you two rarely have sex..." My radar of whether two people were getting naked together was much more accurate than when and if they'd stopped.

"It's been years. Years and years."

"Why are you still married to him?"

"Financial and habitual co-dependence." She tried to smile.

"Did you ever like me? As a friend even? Or was I just the one person you thought wouldn't leave you... and then when I did, however briefly, you plotted to destroy me..."

"Oh, Athena... I was eighteen not a criminal mastermind. Travis was the boy who never liked me back and then my best friend in her baggy sweat-shirts who I thought only pretended to like boys because her mom didn't want her to be a lesbian somehow makes the hottest boy in Illinois fall in love with her with a pretty poem and a tight shirt. I wanted your attention, so yeah, what better way to get a girl's attention than by sleeping with her boyfriend?"

"And then marrying him and stealing my book?"

"You wouldn't talk to me. So I clung to Travis because he was all I had left of you..."

"Come on, Elizabeth. You're not the romantic."

"Or I was a teenage girl with abandonment issues being controlled by a beautiful boy who promised he'd never abandon me. You know Travis... he just has this way of making you do everything he wants."

That I knew. "So..."

"So..."

Took a deep breath. Then, as the delusion of a small life in this small cabin with her disappeared, I explained everything I knew: "Your hotel is failing. You need an investor but they all want to take control away from you. But the *Confessions* sequel money could save you. Save the hotel. Except Travis can't write the book. You tell him to find someone to help him. You give him permission to sleep with other women as long as it's not me. But none of them work. You're desperate for money. Travis is desperate to get his book written. But he's not holding up his end and you're running out of time. So sensing a wedge, Derek Shapiro of Cornell University promises Travis money or time if he helps Derek steal the hotel..."

"Derek? You're sure?"

"I assumed you knew about Derek."

"Nope."

I continued, "You've got a failing business, a failing marriage, and a predatory buyer. And then, and only then, do you tell Travis that you'll invite me out here… and he should seduce me into writing the book with him and then into his bed. Or into his bed and then into the book."

Elizabeth smiled. "The Witchy West Wisdom never fails."

"As much as I'd like that to be true, in this case, it didn't take much wisdom. Just paying attention."

"You're not going to write it with him, are you?"

"You know he's a narcissistic manipulator better than anyone and you still want me in bed with him. Creatively and literally."

"I want…" Elizabeth couldn't hold her eyes on me. Too much shame reflected back at her from my own. "I *need* the sequel money or the hotel is doomed."

"Sell the hotel. Start over. Without Travis."

"All the buyers disappeared two weeks ago. I assumed someone at the bank showed them my bleeding accounts. But Travis probably showed Derek our books which makes much more sense. So now the potential buyers know they could just wait out my demise. Then scoop up the hotel for pennies on the dollar."

"Sell it for pennies. At least you'll be free."

"When I was kid I lived in a fancy apartment filled with breakable things and more breakable people. Then I lived in my cousins' house that smelled like a Costco and then I wandered in the wilderness that is Travis' shadow for years and years... but when I saw this hotel, I knew it was home. The sea. The air. The mountains that will never leave me. I paid for it with every dollar I'd ever had, but also I paid for it with my heart... maybe the first time I ever truly risked my heart for anything..." Elizabeth ran out of words but her glistening eyes finished what they could not.

I have an idea.

Oh, no.

Yes.

No.

Athena...

No!

Sorry!

· · ·

"Elizabeth..."

"Yes, Athena?"

The night her father told her that he was re-marrying a much, *much* younger woman, Elizabeth drove over to my house. January sophomore year. A month before Travis detonated our lives. I wrapped her in my arms as she stepped out of her car. She cried. I cried. We cuddled on the couch and watched my mom's favorite movie, *Steel Magnolias,* which made us cry more. Which made us hold each other tighter. Fell asleep. Woke with her spooning me from behind. Her nose and eyelashes tickling my neck. *Elizabeth...* I remembering whispering. She didn't answer. *I love you...* Did I say it or think it? Can't remember. But she definitely said, *I love you, Athena...* and I pretended not to hear it and went back to sleep. Then Travis happened then I disappeared from her life for a year and then she broke my heart...

. . .

I asked, "How much is the sequel deal worth?"

"One point eight."

"You get half?"

"Yep."

"Can you save the hotel with nine hundred k?"

"If my accountant can do some magic, maybe it buys me a year to fix the problems."

"Fire Derek. Like by text. This second. Tell Travis you want a divorce. Like now. By text. Tell him I'll write the sequel but he can't help me and he can't be near me. Tell him he can get all the credit and his half but that you and I don't want to speak to him ever again."

"I'll give you half of my half. You can stay here at the hotel while you write…"

"If you can barely save the hotel with nine-hundred thousand you definitely can't save it with four-fifty. And if I stay here, you'll seduce me and I'll fall in love with you and then we'll remember we don't trust each other and neither of us will ever stop being broken hearted teenagers."

"Athena…"

"Give me like, what, 5% of the hotel? Is that a lot or a little for investing four hundred and fifty thousand into a dying hotel?"

"It's worth nothing if the hotel fails… if I turn it

around, it could be a lot... but you'll deserve even more."

"5% then. Do we have a deal?"

She took out her phone, sent two texts. "Just fired Derek and divorced Travis. Well, might not be quite official. But yes, that's my way of saying we have a deal."

"Proud of you," I said.

"Why would you do this?"

"Because I love you... as a friend."

She laughed. "Is that *your* way of telling me you don't want to kiss me right now?"

"It's my way of saying that I'm sorry I didn't kiss you in high school but also that I don't think we're meant to kiss each other as adults."

"Can we hug?"

"Yes... after we sign some official looking document and in public and during the day and with at least a million other people around."

She nodded. Sadness tinted with possibility.

"Bye, Elizabeth..."

"Bye, Athena..." As I opened the cabin door, she said, "you were wrong about one detail. I wanted Travis to call you about writing the sequel for years. Maybe because I knew you were the only person who could write it. Maybe because I wanted an excuse for you to be back in my life. But he said he wouldn't be able to control you. Turns out Travis was right about at least one thing."

"Maybe..." And yet I almost fell back under his spell.

"Maybe his powers of persuasion don't last as long as they did when we were young."

"No, they definitely don't."

Ohhhhhhhhhh crap.

It hit me a like a large, loose lightbulb falling from a tall ceiling.

"What is it?" Elizabeth asked.

I said, "I do need to talk to Travis one last time after all. Where would he be?"

"The old caretakers house. Technically that's where we live together. But I usually stay here. Just take the stone path down and then along the hotel and past the tennis courts."

"Okay. Thanks." Turned to leave again.

"Athena, can I ask what you need to say to him?"

"Just need to heal one last wound from my youth."

"Okay. Good luck."

Without thinking, I kissed my hand and blew it at her. Unlike Travis, my air-kiss aim was impeccable. "Don't catch that!"

But she ignored my command, caught it, and brought it tenderly to her cheek.

I'm no longer young or ambitious, so my tears were pouring by the time I stepped back outside.

Saturday Morning

COFFEE
WITH
DETECTIVE BLUE

7:59 AM

Chapter Twenty-Eight

HAD to wipe tears from the memory. If I was an actor, I'd win an award for my impeccable timing. If I was an actor, the tears would also be cinematic and delicate and even attractive. But these tears would leave red splotches and instigate a runny nose. Not helpful in my quest to kiss that mustache.

Detective Blue reluctantly sympathized at my first sign of sadness. He fought it with, "And I suppose you're going to tell me *that* was the last time you saw Elizabeth Diaz alive." Blue had sunken into his chair as my story had unraveled his theory.

"You know it was."

"You remain my prime suspect."

"Ah. But no longer your only suspect. We're making progress." I winked.

"I, uh…"

"It's okay, Detective Blue. If the roles were reversed, you would have been my prime suspect, too." Mostly because I was so attracted to him. But he didn't need to hear that now.

"I do need to step out and check on a few things, Ms. West."

"Derek didn't tell you about being fired and there's no chance Travis told you about the divorce text."

"You, uh…"

"It's okay. Go on."

"You have a visitor that I'm going to let in. She's been asking to see you since five a.m. and has been threatening, well, everyone."

"Of course she has."

My biggest critic and fiercest defender are the same person. I know I'm not the only one.

. . .

"Hello, mother," I said as Nancy West bulldozed into the hotel back office that had been home for what seemed like a couple lifetimes. "How'd you get out here so fast?"

"I was on a plane at three p.m. Chicago time yesterday."

"So you have so little faith in me that you flew out even before I was a suspect in the death of my high school best friend?"

"Shhh. Not another word. I called a lawyer in Beverly Hills. He's gotten a lot of celebrities cleared of assault charges so he must be really good — "

"Sounds like a great guy. But I don't need a lawyer."

"I will not see my daughter waste the rest of her life in jail after wasting far too much of it already!"

"Thanks, mom."

"You know what I mean."

"Oh, I know... but Blue doesn't think I did it anymore."

"Blue? The Detective? Please tell me you haven't been too familiar with him."

"I only asked him to lunch once."

"Athena!"

"He said no."

"Because only a guilty person would ask a detective to lunch during an interrogation!"

"I'd like to think no other guilty or not-guilty person would do it besides me. I need one unique talent I and I alone am capable of."

Before my mother could raise her aghast-ness from level 9 to level 10, Blue walked back in. "Sorry about that."

Before I could speak, my mother shot, "My daughter will not say another word without a lawyer present!"

"Oh, I'm definitely going to say a lot of words." I winked at Blue. He (sorta) didn't (maybe) even mind this time.

Friday Night

outside the
Desmond
Diamond
Hotel

12:33 AM

(Again, technically, Early Saturday Morning)

Chapter Twenty-Nine

AFTER WALKING AWAY from Elizabeth I couldn't stop crying and assumed I'd just cry for the rest of time. Like I'd have to eat and sleep and even poop while crying. I didn't even mind the prospect. Maybe I'd break the world record for longest cry and my life would finally have meaning.

Yet the waterfall slowed the further I got away and managed to wipe my face clean of tears by the time I passed by the tennis courts. Steeled myself for Travis's seduction offensive as I knocked on a two story house that would be more at home on a 1980s sitcom than on the grounds of a glamorous coastal hotel.

My former first boyfriend and hopefully Elizabeth's soon-to-be former husband answered the door in an orange speedo underwear and nothing else.

It's shocking how many men find themselves irresistible in various forms of undress while far too many women feel undesirable unless presented like Cinderella at the ball.

"Beautiful Athena..." he cooed. "Come in, come in..."

But as he spoke, my eyes fell on his bare belly-button. Now this might sound incredibly superficial but Travis Diaz, once owner of a body fantasized by Calvin Klein marketing executives, had, at thirty-five, an 'innie' belly-button. The first time I saw his bare body, I was in awe of his 'outie'. To me and my layered mid-section, this was some kind of miracle of genetic magic. But at this moment I found it very profound that Travis's belly-button could not out duel father time any better than the rest of us.

"Athena... *Athena*..."

I looked up. Was my body chemistry... unmoved? My goodness. Maybe there's hope for me yet.

"What's wrong? Come in. Let's discuss why you haven't started working on the book yet..."

"I'm not coming in, Travis. And I won't be able to see you again. Like ever again. But I will write the sequel for you. Well, not for you. I don't need my name on it. I don't need anything from you except two small things: One, grant Elizabeth her divorce. And two, move out of the hotel and never contact Diana again."

"Who?" His mouth lied as his face confessed the truth.

"Travis. Please. You need me to write this far more than you need a young woman worshipping you. She's also too talented a writer to be letting you vampire her time and talent."

"I don't know who this Diana is and I don't know how you read her work — "

"The sequel document you sent. You didn't write a word of it. She did. And she thinks she's in love with you. And she thinks you're meant to be her romantic lover and creative partner until after the afterlife. But she doesn't know she's a bit player in your story. Just like you don't know your story isn't a hero's arc... it's a villain's."

"You've become very jaded and angry, Athena. I really don't think you're the right mother for our baby anymore."

"Well, *Confessions* is half owned by Elizabeth and she thinks I am. And for someone who loves calling himself an artist you hate doing the actual work of creating art far too much to ever finish the book without me.”

I knew this was a kill shot at the very deluded self image of a narcissistic man. But, my goodness, I was not prepared for the eyes bulging and veins vibrating and saliva bubbling at the corners of his disappearing lips. This de-evolving man then hissed:

"Athena, I made you. You were a frumpy, badly dressed underclassman who wrote one good poem... I turned you into something meaningful. I made you beautiful. *I* made *you* a writer. Maybe you wrote the dumb book, but I inspired you to write it. Which is far more important. Anyone can write a book! The people that inspire are the much more important ones. THAT'S why I'm so much more important than you! YOU'RE A TYPIST! I'M THE ARTIST!”

"Cool. Cool. This is better than I thought." Showed him my phone.

"What are you doing?"

"Recording you. Don't worry. I won't show

anyone. I mean, I *definitely* will show everyone if you lie to anyone about me or manipulate Elizabeth or even look at Diana ever again. But as long as you behave, no one needs to know you're a total fraud."

He lunged at me. And I hated touching him in any way, but I had no choice but to unleash a high, fast knee right into the heart of that orange speedo.

He fell fast. Knees hit first, that once perfect face followed with a thump against the cement stoop. For a moment, I felt like I could stop a speeding bullet and leap tall buildings and stop eating cookies before bed every night. But then as I watched my first love pathetically moan on the ground, I ached for all the years I wasted on him. All the love I held back or spent too easily after him. I had finally caught my Moby Dick and it felt not triumphant but like I had spent my life chasing a dumb fucking fish.

Chapter Thirty

DRIFTED BACK along the stone path, this time toward the front entrance to the hotel.

Derek Shapiro of Cornell University fast stepped into my face the moment my feet touched the lobby tile. He wasn't subtle: "If this messes up my plans, which it won't because you're a dumb, ugly woman, but if it does, I'll kill you."

Didn't have it in me to knee a second asshole in the genitals not even an hour into the new day, so I said, "Derek, good luck spending the rest of your life hating the world for favoring strong women and sensitive men over the likes of you."

Processing long sentences wasn't his strong suit which left him flat footed as I pushed on toward the elevator. Waiting there was Lilith Lennon.

I said, "You and Derek certainly aren't afraid of confrontation."

But Lilith wasn't stewing with juvenile vengeance like her counterpart. Instead, her whole body was breaking along with her broken heart. Less visceral, but perhaps more dangerous. "Elizabeth's my world."

"She was once mine," I said.

"I'd rather be dead then end up like you."

Listen, I'm the first one to acknowledge my low self-esteem and dalliances with depression. But my life wasn't *that* terrible, right? Not the time to tell Lilith that. So I could only offer,

"The only person responsible for your happiness is you. I didn't truly realize that until today. You figure that out at your age, I promise you won't end up like me."

Lilith was much brighter than Derek, but my penchant for speaking in inorganic literary flourishes left a second Desmond Diamond employee frozen in my wake.

Stepped into the elevator and waved good-bye

to Lilith, hoping that her hurt didn't lead her to hurt herself or anyone else.

When the elevator opened on my floor, a figure was standing at my door. I knew what they wanted. I probably wanted the same thing. Had about twenty seconds to decide if this would be a small mistake or massive one.

Because there was no question it would definitely, *definitely* be a mistake.

Saturday Morning

COFFEE
WITH
DETECTIVE BLUE
(And Mom)

8:18 AM

Chapter Thirty-One

MY MOTHER and Detective Blue both tilted their heads and raised their eyebrows simultaneously. A broad shouldered, mustached black man in his mid-thirties and an unfairly thin sixty-two year old white woman — for the briefest of moments — looked like twins. (Oh-my-god-I-better-not-be-attracted-to-my-mother.)

"What?" I said even though I knew why each was holding their breath. Instead of letting either state the obvious, I turned to Blue and asked, "Do you have all our suspects still on hotel grounds?"

"Yes, I mean... no... I mean... why?"

"Well, now that my mother is here, I'd like to demonstrate that her daughter is not incompetent at everything. Just most things."

"What do you mean!?" My mother protested.

Blue was equally confused, just less exasperated, "I have the same question your mother does."

"My mom loves mystery novels. And some of her favorite detectives often revealed the killer with all the central suspects in the same room."

My mom's anxiety took on new colors. "Athena I really don't think you understand how real life works."

"That's probably true, mom. But I understand how people's minds work. And I understand that Blue has no idea who killed Elizabeth and that he's desperate enough to let me have a moment so he can find out."

Mom twisted her head fast toward Blue. But he kept his gaze on me. That's when I saw it. Felt it. The chemistry. It was always there. But for the first time he didn't fight it. I knew what he was going to say. So did he. But he wanted to indulge in our shared moment. So I didn't mind he didn't speak right away.

My mother did. She was ready to explode.

Blue finally broke our savored tension with, "Okay, Ms. West. I feel like I owe you for not seeing more than I wanted to see the past few hours. What do you need from me?"

Saturday Morning

~~COFFEE~~
KILLER REVEAL
WITH
DETECTIVE BLUE
(And Mom
& Travis & Lilith & Derek & Zai)

8:37 AM

Chapter Thirty-Two

Blue and one of his uniformed officers led mom and me out of the back office, across an empty lobby, and into a windowless conference room.

There were five oval tables. Travis, Lilith, Derek, and Zai all sat at different ones as if they feared guilt was contagious. A second uniformed officer stood at the back of the room. Directed my mother to sit at the fifth and only empty table.

Blue closed the conference room door behind us then stepped beside me. "This is Athena West. My department has hired her as consulting detective on this case."

. . .

onsulting detective? Like *Sherlock Holmes, Consulting Detective*, Consulting Detective? Did a man I fancied just champion and elevate me at great personal and professional risk?

My god. What I had to say just became that much more devastating.

"Hi," I said. A little twelve year-old new girl to the class vibe. That's okay. Shook it off. "First, thank you, Detective Blue. Second, can I have a word in private before I begin?"

He nodded, stepped toward the door, his back now to the room. I stepped beside him.

Whispered what I needed to whisper.

Blue nodded again, spoke to one of the officers. That officer left the room as I again stepped to the center.

. . .

"Hi... again. While it's just been lovely being insulted, assaulted, seduced, and doubted by all of you over the past 15 hours, all good times must come to an end. Each of you has the anger, ego, or motive to kill someone. But our legal system is set up only to punish the crimes people actually commit and not the ones you long for in your heart..."

I thought that was a pretty good start. My mother, however, was already bored. She was spinning her finger, the evergreen hand gesture to *get the fuck on with it*.

So I did, "Derek Shapiro of Cornell University —" his body twisted even as it petrified, "— your very privileged rich kid plan to drive the hotel into bankruptcy where you could steal it in foreclosure is as lame as it is immoral. Gosh, I wish you had to spend the rest of your life behind bars if only to save young women from enduring your out-dated sexism and creepy charms. But, alas, when I stepped out into the hall at half past two a.m. I looked down into the lobby and found you pacing in the same place I left you ninety-minutes before. I am absolutely sure you wanted to kill Elizabeth and me and every other woman who has wronged you. But today was not the day you went through with it."

Despite my declaring his innocence, Derek debated in that limited brain of his the pros and cons of leaping from the table and choking me out. But I turned my attention forever away from him and towards,

"Lilith," I said. "As someone who loved Elizabeth a long time ago and then fantasized about her death long after she broke my heart, I relate to all the pain her cold ends to hot beginnings inspire. Your brain tells you it will be easier to kill the pain with rage than heal the pain with distance. When I first met you, I must admit, I thought you were my favorite to play the bad guy in whatever the weekend story wrote. You did leave the cabin after Elizabeth broke up with you to find Derek and finally take him up on his offer to steal the hotel from your now ex-lover. Sadly funny how you and Derek were each other's alibi at the time of the murder. Could he have killed Elizabeth? In another time and place yes. Could you have? I don't think so... your biggest crime was falling in love with a woman whose ability to love ended where her abandonment issues began." Lilith wanted to hate me for saying this, but instead turned away from the others, buried her face in her hands and tried her best to muffle her sobs. Her best was terrible. The sobs were really, really loud. But we collectively pretended they weren't.

Took a deep breath. Can I skip this part?
Sure.
No, I can't.
Yes. Think of Blue.
I can't hide this from him.
If you don't hide it from Blue, your love story will end before it begins.
Sorry.
ATHENA! DON'T SAAAAAAA —-

"Zai." Looked at him for the first time since entering the room. Sorta wanted to puke. Should I puke? Maybe if I puke I won't have to admit this.

"Hi, Athenaaaaaa." He was grinning. Everyone must know by now. Time to rip off the band-aid.

"For a long time I assumed Travis had cut off the security cameras. But even for a man burdened by obviousness, Travis would have known had he cut those off, the police would have an easy thread to connect him to the murder..."

"B-but Athenaaaaa," Zai stuttered. Sweat pooled in his temples. Even his dimples. "I d-did that so Elizabeth wouldn't know a-bout... You kno-know... You sa-said, you no-know..."

"I know. Zai, you didn't kill Elizabeth because at one am you were..." Looked toward Blue. He should see the shame in my eyes. Maybe that would help him get over it. "... you were waiting outside my hotel room. And then you and I went inside that hotel room and... well, some people self-medicate with alcohol, others with drugs, and some of us self-medicate with getting naked with strangers we should never get naked with. To distract ourselves from recent romantic wounds and long term emotional scars. So Zai, trying to forget Elizabeth, and I, trying to forget Elizabeth, Travis, and decades of mistakes I made because of them, self-medicated with each other..."

"Twice," Zaid said. Somehow he didn't stumble over that.

"Yes, Zai... twice..." I said and had to turn away from Blue. The level of shame in my eyes was too large for any other human to endure the sight of. Spun toward my mother. "I want everyone to know that I'm also trying to self-medicate with sugar more often. Not as good an option as yoga or green tea or whatever else people without an absent father, a controlling mother, and teenage emotional trauma do, but better than what I did last night..."

Blue said, "Let's move on."

Goodness that felt loaded with double meaning. Don't cry. "Yes, okay, let's move on to..." As my eyes fell on Travis the urge to cry was subdued by the desire to avenge. Avenge Elizabeth's death. Avenge the stolen sixteen years. "Travis... even as a sophomore in high school, I knew you were a narcissist. Frankly, narcissists think they can hide in plain sight but narcissism is way too into itself to not plant a big neon sign on your forehead that screams, 'Proud Narcissist Inside'. Sorry, Mom..."

"Why are you apologizing to me!?" My mother exclaimed. Then it hit her. "Oh..." And she fell into silence. A place she rarely fell.

I turned back toward Travis. His face shifted with every blink of his eyes. One second he's that descended-from-the-heavens teenage dream I fell in love with a lifetime ago. The next second his face contorts into the pathetic, demonic creature in the orange speedo from last night.

Chapter Thirty-Three

(YEARS AGO)

FROM THE FIRST date on the beach, all I wanted to do with Travis was breathe as few breaths without him as possible. Drive to school together? Of course. Walk to class together, go to lunch together, go home with him? Yes, yes, and yes. Anything he wanted to do, I'd do it as long as it was together. So when he first suggested writing a book together I said yes because I would have said yes to anything.

But one 'yes' above any other has haunted me ever since.

It was a Sunday night. It had been a long weekend dealing with my dad, his Stepford second wife, and my wannabe Nazi stepbrothers. All I wanted to do was cuddle with the love of my life and watch something that allowed my dead brain to stay dead. But Travis demanded we write. But this always meant me writing. Me typing. Me making the tortured, soul draining effort to dig into the heads of our characters and find truth and dialogue and drama. He'd just sit there, mumbling his, 'Oh this is so good, we're gonna be famous, this book is so good…' But that Sunday night. I couldn't. I could have swam across all the Great Lakes before I could do the creative work to write anything of worth. To my refusal, Travis said, "If you can't write with me, you can't be with me." There was no joy or warmth in his words. It was a threat.

My entire life had been constructed around him. If Travis left me, I was sure I would die. Sure of it. So I wrote that night. And every night he asked.

But what if I hadn't?

If I had said, 'I can't' write, Travis. I can't perform for you.' I truly believe Travis would have left me. And, despite my fears, I would have survived. And Elizabeth would have survived last night.

Chapter Thirty-Four

"Travis," I said, "I don't need to re-cap for the room the depths of your fraud…"

The conference room door cracked open. The officer who had left returned. Behind him was Diana. My younger doppelgänger inside and out. My daughter from another universe. Her eyes as lost as they were last night. When I told her to give her lover one more chance. When my Witchy West Wisdom failed us all.

The officer sat Diana next to my mother. The familiarity would be impossible for a stranger not to sense, but my mother felt it almost as deeply as I.

This was a young woman who could be our family. Mom took Diana's shaking hand in her own. I always felt if I had kids, they would be spared Nancy West's impossible expectations and would instead thrive in her unbreakable love.

"...**B**ut here's the thing I didn't understand, Travis... I thought you merely a fraud with romance and art. I couldn't or wouldn't see that you can't even express your malice without help from others."

"What the hell are you talking about?" He turned to Blue. "She's gonna make up some crazy things. I didn't say or do any of it."

"Oh, don't worry," I said. "I already showed Detective Blue the video I took of you last night. But you don't care that Detective Blue knows you didn't write the book. Detective Blue doesn't care you didn't write the book. Detective Blue only cares if you murdered Elizabeth..."

"I DIDN'T!" He screamed like a five year-old who didn't actually know what he was being accused of.

Turned away from Travis, stepped to the table that held mom and Diana. I crouched in front of

Diana. Took the hand my mother didn't hold into my own. My eyes met hers. In them I found my younger self. I wanted to protect her. Fight for her. Lie for her. But lying to myself had never helped me and it wouldn't help Diana either. "Diana…"

"I'm sorry."

"Don't say anything. Okay? I don't even want you to nod. I just want you to sit there. And then we'll do everything we can to help. Okay?"

"Okay."

"That's my fault. Don't even say okay. Okay?"

She didn't open her mouth or move her head.

"Good job. At some point in my last conversation with Elizabeth, it hit me that you didn't go home after I walked you to your car. You had gone back to Travis because I know as well as you that once Travis's romantic, gaslighting hooks are inside you, it's almost impossible to break free. And you probably went back in that mini-skirt and Travis had done what every average asshole male does when a woman deliriously desperate to regain his attention shows up on his doorstep. But one of my many mistakes last night was that I assumed when Travis answered in his underwear and invited me inside that you had left. I had hoped he already dumped you for the final time. That you'd be free. But the reality is you were still in the caretaker's house with Travis. He had likely hidden you in the bathroom."

Diana wanted to confirm this. I shook my head before she could.

"If I had fallen back under his spell — under his manipulative control — I could have easily been talked into entering that house. Into having sex with Travis. And you would have had to listen to the man who told you he loved you more than the universe itself be with another women inches from where he had imprisoned you."

Diana's shaking spread from hands to arms to lips to pupils.

"But instead I left Travis with a wounded groin and a more wounded ego. And you came out of the bathroom and could only see the man you loved. You believed him when he said you would write a book together and you would be famous and your love would re-write the laws of what love could be. But last night, just before one a.m., he said something not too different from, "She's going to stop us from being together. She's going to keep our book from being in the world."

I begged Diana's eyes not to nod. Instead they

cried. Those tears confessed more than a nod could have.

"Travis then said something like 'I can't see you again until she's gone forever'."

I was pressing my reveal to my most ambitious end. I had to. For Diana's sake. For Elizabeth's. For my own.

"This is all insane!" Travis cried out. Whined. Bitched. No woman has ever deserved that insult more than Travis and all men like him.

Blue mouthed, *that's enough.*

"One more question," I said to them both, then turned to Travis. "When you told Diana you couldn't be with her until 'she' was gone forever. Did you mean Elizabeth... or me?"

Oh, Travis wanted to say it. He wanted to let me know it should have been me who was dead. I could see the word form in his eyes. See his lips part ever so.

Please, Travis. Please admit it was me. Please confess to manipulating Diana into murder and spend your life in jail trapped with a bunch of ugly men who would love a man as pretty as you.

But he caught himself. He was a villain who wasn't ready for his story to end. So instead his mouth opened for, "I would like a lawyer," and didn't say another word.

Epilogue

As one of the officers read Diana her rights and placed the handcuffs around her wrists, my mother cried. Something she had never done over me.

The second officer asked Travis to come with him to the station for additional questioning. As they walked out, the man who had lorded over far too much of my life promised, "Our story isn't over, Athena."

He was right. Wished he wasn't. But what Travis didn't understand was that Athena West was now the main character of this story. And Travis Diaz would be nothing more than an occasional guest star that everyone was rooting against.

. . .

I reminded Lilith Lennon that Elizabeth had fired Derek which left her in charge of the Desmond Diamond Hotel. "It's what she would have wanted," I said. Lilith had no more tears to offer, nodded a thank you, and disappeared into the hotel.

Zai hugged me the first chance he could. He lingered. Like *really* lingered. Reminded myself that I'm really, *really* good in bed and that he might be having more feelings than a usual one night stand might justify. "Zai," I started.

"Atheeeeeenaaaa." He was really cute. But puppy cute.

"Lilith will need a lot of help in the days to come. Can you be there for her?"

"Yes. Anything you want." Then lingered again.

"Zai…"

"Atheeeenaaaa…."

"Lilith went that way." I pointed. And as if I threw a tennis ball, Zai raced out of view.

· · ·

Detective Blue stood near the exit to the conference room. Arms crossed. Which made his biceps look really big and made his chest look just the right shape to lay my head against. Ached to race the last ten feet between us. He would open his arms, envelope me, and we'd be naming our children by dinner.

Instead I walked. Sorta like a normal person might walk.

"Well done, Ms. West."

"You probably would have preferred I just tell you in the back room."

"Nah. I enjoyed it. A lot. The biggest downside will be spending the rest of my career finding an end to a case as memorable as this one."

"Me, too."

"You planning on becoming a detective now?"

"Well, a consulting detective. It suits me. All the interesting stuff I'm good at and none of the boring stuff like paperwork and rules and proof."

"Don't know if our department will have that many cases worthy of your skills."

"You'll find a few. You'll also recommend me to other departments and then those departments will recommend me and so on until I'm practically famous. Don't worry, you'll always be my first and favorite case."

"Did you know from the start? Was it all just having fun with me?"

"Oh. No. Sorry you thought that. My confession of 'sorta' was true at the moment and still true now. If I had made five other choices last night, especially with Diana, Elizabeth would be alive. But to understand who actually wielded the knife, I had to talk through the night, remember every detail. I had to see it again and see it through your eyes to stay objective."

"That makes me feel... less useless."

"You were very, very useful, Detective Blue."

The word useful never had so many uses.

To that, Blue said, "You, um, asked me to lunch... I know that was just you having fun, but — "

"It wasn't. Our chemistry is real. I knew it the

instant I saw you. Our brains like each other, too. Our hearts probably would as well."

"I am…"

"Married. I know. Separated. Three months?"

"Five."

"You two were college sweat hearts. No, law school. But you decided to become a detective. That annoyed her. She's a big corporate lawyer. Makes a lot more money than you. She can't get pregnant and was feeling inadequate so she cheated on you. Some rich jerk at her law firm. She feels terrible. She begs for forgiveness every day. You haven't slept with anyone since so you're starting to think that means you should give her another chance."

B lue wanted to kiss me. His eyes. His lips. His brain barely held back his arms from grabbing me. Gosh, I wanted that mustache against my mouth. Once I kissed him, don't know if I'd ever be able to kiss someone else. But instead of kissing me, he asked,

· · ·

"How do you do that?"

"So I got everything right?"

"You got enough right."

"Faces — especially eyes — tell me stories. I like stories. So I pay attention."

"I have to go to the station. The Travis Diaz aspect of this will require my time. But if you're free tonight, maybe dinner..."

"Blue."

"Name is Keenan."

"Detective Blue. I hated having to tell you about my night with Zai — "

"I don't care."

"I know you don't. But you don't care because you don't realize that if I met you for dinner tonight I wouldn't be able to stop from kissing you and I just know I'm going to like kissing you and then we'll make love and you'll love making love to me and think that means you're in love with me and then you'll think you're over your wife until one day you realize you're not and I'll be the rebound and our chemistry — and how our story began — is too great for me to be the rebound and for you to be another Zai."

I wanted him to tell me I was wrong. Tell me all

the reasons we should ignore logic and our probable romantic doom and leap into each other tonight or this very second. But instead Detective Blue said, "You got one thing wrong earlier. I don't like your brain. I love it."

No man had ever said that to me.
Don't cry.
I love him.
You love what love could be with him.
I want our story to start today.
It did start today. Chapter two can wait.

"Detective Blue," I said as I held out my hand. He took it in his own. "I look forward to our next case together."
He smiled. "Me, too, Detective West."

He just called me Detective West. Get me the fuck out of here before I cry and leap into his arms and kiss him and —

. . .

"Mother," I said, "Time to go." Fifteen minutes later, we were in an Uber back toward LAX. Once the Desmond Diamond Hotel disappeared behind us, I said, "See? Your daughter's not an idiot with everything."

My mother took my hand in hers. While looking anywhere but at me, she said, "When you were eight, we were in the dining room. At home. The four of us. Last time the four of us had dinner together. I had made pot roast. I hated pot roast. You said to your father, 'Dad, why are you hiding secrets in your wrinkles?' He laughed. He thought you were cute. But that's when I knew. Not just that your dad was cheating on me, but that my daughter could see things no one else could. That you were special. But I'm a mother who only knows how to protect. So I tried to make my special girl fit in instead of helping her stand out."

Those words broke me in the best, most brutal way. I sunk then collapsed my head into my mother's lap and sobbed. For the years behind me wasted on Travis. For the years ahead I might never have with Blue. For all Diana would never be. And most of all for all Elizabeth would never see.

The End

About the Authors

When **Dr Catherine Gottfred** was twelve years-old, she debated whether to become a writer or a doctor. Determining that all the famous writers she knew were depressed, she got her PhD in Speech and Language... and yet still spent most of her life wrestling what she romantically refers to as "existential despair."

Dr. Gottfred founded the non-profit Language-Empowers-All-People (LEAP) in 1986, dedicated to providing researched-based language/literacy development to children, families, home visitors, and teachers. LEAP developed a free app, Beginning-With-Babble, giving daily age-appropriate language tips to parents. Language-Through-Science, Language-for-Emergent Readers, and Language-for-Scholars are examples of programs LEAP provides in Chicago and shares nationally. Dr. Gottfred taught at Northwestern, Illinois, and Northern Illinois universities, and worked clinically in private practice, hospitals, and schools. She was

President of ASHA and ISHA and ASHA's VP of Government Affairs. She served on the Chicago Charter School Board, Rush University ComD Advisory Board, Advocate Hospitals Foundation Board and Institutional Review Board, DePauw University Visitors Board, Glenbrook Multicultural Committee, Glenview Education Association Board, Daniel Murphy Scholarship Board, and Chicago-Youth-Centers Lower-North Board. Dr. Gottfred has received ASHA and ISHA Fellow, ISHA Honors, DiCarlo Award-Outstanding Clinical Achievement, Kleffner Lifetime Clinical Career Award, Northwestern University School of Communications Alumni of the Year in 2010, and was named one of 26 Trailblazer Alumnae Who Changed the World by Northwestern University School of Communication.

b.t. gottfred grew up witnessing his mother read every free moment she had from her career and kids. Often a mystery book. Usually Agatha Christie. While he never had to work to get her attention quite like Athena worked to get Nancy West's, his mother's passion for words both spoken and written inspired his life's eclectic literary path.

Gottfred is a novelist, screenwriter, producer, director, and playwright who has penned critically-acclaimed novels that explore themes such as gender, sexuality, and human relationships. Starred reviews from Kirkus Reviews, Booklist, Publishers Weekly, and VOYA, Noted reviewers have called his books "swoon inducing and heartbreaking" (School Library Journal), "hilarious and deeply honest" (Publishers Weekly) and "plainly a talent to watch" (Kirkus). His work has been selected as one of Book-Riot's Best of the Decade, Audible's Best of the Year, and has also been featured in the New York Times, Bustle, 60 Minutes, and Salon. His plays have been produced around the country, his films have been shown around the world.

In his last novel, THE NEXT GOD, he explores the very personal and universal search for spiritual purpose through the eyes of a college sophomore traveling to Indiana to see if a man claiming to be a god actually is one.

ATHENA WEST WILL RETURN IN ANOTHER CRAZY COZY MURDER MYSTERY

www.ingramcontent.com/pod-product-compliance
Lightning Source LLC
Chambersburg PA
CBHW061346310726
48974CB00001B/217